THE IRON ROADS

ailroad company was set to press for
o-south route through Montana,
v and Jesse Brannin had recently
what was the only linking track
through the timberline of the
Mountains. The town that
on the venture was called Whisper,
it from dying under the squeeze
mpany's business might, something
done. Townsfolk and loyal
n were seconded to fight – but it
ough. The Brannins had to find a
to beat off the assault of those
the rail bosses had sent ahead of their
k layers.

THE IRON ROADS

THE IRON ROADS

by

Caleb Rand

Dales Large Print Books
Long Preston, North Yorkshire,
BD23 4ND, England.

British Library Cataloguing in Publication Data.

Rand, Caleb
  The iron roads.

    A catalogue record of this book is
    available from the British Library.

    ISBN   978-1-84262-616-0 pbk

First published in Great Britain 2007 by Robert Hale Limited

Copyright © Caleb Rand 2007

Cover illustration © Gordon Crabb by arrangement with
Alison Eldred

The right of Caleb Rand to be identified as the author of this
work has been asserted by him in accordance with the
Copyright, Designs and Patents Act, 1988

Published in Large Print 2008 by arrangement with
Robert Hale Ltd.

Dales Large Print is an imprint of Library Magna Books Ltd.

Printed and bound in Great Britain by
T.J. (International) Ltd., Cornwall, PL28 8RW

For the illustrator, friend and wife,
Raphilena Margaret ...
love and many thanks

1

It was a raw, early spring afternoon, and the north-bound train to Garrison had just clanked and snorted from the station. The swell of anticipation that always attended its arrival and departure subsided, and Pony Flats settled down to its dull, everyday way of life. It usually stayed that way until the south-bound to Butte City arrived just before five o'clock.

With his collar turned up against the wind, Lemuel Essex came riding up the street. As sheriff he made it his business to meet the four local trains a day that passed through. Essex was middle-aged, had been around, seen a bit, and wasn't too disposed to worry. But then, this parcel of Montana had settled down to orderly living, and other than a little rustling and an occasional fight among labourers on the branch lines of the Northern Pacific Rail Road, nothing much happened around Pony Flats to give him any real concern.

Leaning against one of the uprights that

held up the wooden canopy of Buffers Saloon, Duff Chapter was watching the sheriff with a deceptive lack of concentration. Inside, standing to one side of the window, was his partner, Gregor Froote.

They had ridden into Pony Flats that morning and tethered their horses at the hitching rail out front of the bank. They looked like a couple of saddle slicks, with their hard-bitten faces. But then northern winters had a habit of putting cruel lines across most peoples' faces if they stayed too long.

A thought ran through Chapter's mind as he eyed the sheriff discreetly. The man wouldn't be wearing top coat and gloves if he was only toing and froing from his office, he told himself.

Just then, as if in response to Chapter's thoughts, a man stepped to the edge of the sidewalk. 'Hey, Sheriff,' he called out. 'I was just comin' round to see you. You not goin' back to your office?'

'No, I'm not,' Essex answered. 'I'm servin' a writ on Ceda Muspratt. I figured to get out there an' back before nightfall. What did you want me for, Harber?'

'Council business. I guess it can wait.'

'I should be back by five,' Essex called

back. 'See me then.'

Duff Chapter pulled a stogie from a top pocket, lit up, and with his head down, stood smoking thoughtfully. But his eyes followed the sheriff, and when he was sure that Essex had ridden straight out the west end of town, he beckoned for Froote to join him.

'Sheriff won't be back for two or three hours,' he said.

Froote, short and tight-featured, nodded sourly. 'Yeah, I heard. So now's as good a time as any.'

The two men sauntered across the street, the pounded dirt kicking up with their footfalls. As they reached the opposite sidewalk, a light freighter stopped in front of the bank and they exchanged a quick glance, pretended to hold their lack of particular interest.

But when the driver struggled with a large wooden filing cabinet, he caught the two men watching him as they fiddled with the tie-reins of their horses.

'Ain't fit work for a man o' my years,' he suggested with a wry smile. 'Everythin' I deliver to this bank weighs heavy. Never get me a bag o' feathers, or one o' them pomandered cushions.'

'You're the wrong end o' town for that

stuff, ol' man. We'll give you a hand,' Chapter volunteered, swinging an empty canvas feed bag on top of the cabinet.

The driver grunted his satisfaction, stood to one side and then held the door open. 'It's your cabinet delivery, Mr Broome,' he called out, following Chapter and Froote into the bank.

The owner of the bank, Wallace Broome, was standing behind the mesh-grilled counter that divided the room. He was talking to two customers. 'Tell them where you want the cabinet, Connor,' he said, turning to his cashier.

Looking around them, Chapter and Froote noticed that the bank's safe was protected by a further partition, but its door was standing open.

'Best put it right in here,' the cashier said, unlocking the back-up grille. 'Easiest for me.'

'OK,' Chapter said, as he and Froote moved through the low door in the counter. They lowered the filing cabinet, and eased it snug to the big, floor-standing safe.

'Thanks, fellers,' the cashier nodded. 'That's very good o' you.

Chapter agreed. 'Yeah, ain't it just. But then we did have a motive,' he said, while methodically pulling his Colt revolver.

Gregor Froote was doing the same. 'Stand very still, an' none o' you gets hurt: *move*, an' you sure as hell will,' he advised everyone sternly. Swiftly he pulled down the bag, and started scooping up dust pokes and paper currency from the cashier's cage. He was lifting packets from the shelves of the safe, when a man appeared unsuspectingly through the bank's double doors.

Chapter cursed. 'Yep, it *really* is happenin' here,' he said with a sharp, snappy grin. He could have fired before the man backed off through the door, but that would have stirred the town, and that wouldn't have helped. Instead, he told Froote to get moving.

Holding Broome and the others at bay, they edged themselves nearer the doors. The man who had walked in on the hold-up, had run to the town's nearby hotel, and now Froote and Chapter saw armed men already converging on the bank.

'Remember, you're small-town businessmen, not gun hands,' Chapter grated. 'An' this situation ain't worth losin' your life over.'

Everyone in the bank understood, slumped their shoulders in acceptance of the explicit warning. Everyone except Eggar Dunstan. He was one of the two customers who had been caught at the counter, and he was understanding something else. Firstly, his user account and his savings were in Wallace Broome's bank, and secondly, he carried a serviceable .44 Colt beneath his coat. As Chapter and Froote made for the door, Dunstan dropped his right hand.

Chapter saw him and shook his head. 'I just got through tellin' you, feller. I already got your money, so you'd be dyin' for nothin'.'

'It's *all* I got. That ain't *nothin'*,' Dunstan said plaintively. He made a futile grab for his Colt, but he was nowhere near proficient enough.

Chapter yelled a curse and put a single bullet low into Dunstan's midriff before the man could even draw back the Colt's hammer.

Now, half-a-dozen men were closing on the bank, as Froote and Chapter ran out and leapt to their saddles. The men were brave enough, but with two bank robbers sitting their horses and resolutely emptying their guns at them, they scattered to convenient doorways and side alleys.

Pulling carbines from their saddle boots, Froote and Chapter spurred their horses along the street. Heading away from indiscriminate volleys of lead, they swept out the east end of town, swung south across the railroad track, and ran hard for the safety of the wasteland beyond.

In the bank, Eggar Dunstan had died doubled-up, clutching his belly. Wallace Broome ran out into the street, yelling, 'Where for the love o' God is Essex?'

'He's gone to Ceda Muspratt's ... won't be back for a few hours yet,' a breathless Harber Gemm informed him.

Hoping to do something for Dunstan, the town doctor, TJ. Mulberry, rushed into the bank. Moments later, he came out shaking his head. 'He's dead. So they can add murder to bank robbery,' he said, deeply angered.

'Why do we have to wait for Lem?' Gemm said. 'I got a saddled horse down the street, an' I can get me a rifle. How many o' you are ready to join me?'

Gemm looked at the raised hands, noted the aggrieved rumblings. 'Good,' he said. 'We can follow the vultures to where them murderin' varmints are headed.'

2

It was the shooting of Eggar Dunstan that gave the posse its guts and grim determination as they rode swiftly from town, heading south towards the distant Beaverheads.

Word was sent out to the sheriff, who hurried back from serving an out-of-town writ. After a quick breakdown of the incident from Wallace Broome, he called the banker and a few others who had witnessed the robbery, back to his office.

'They ain't new to the business,' he said, turning over a file of wanted notices. 'Too sure of 'emselves for that. They'll be here somewhere.'

'That's them,' Broome said, a minute later. He turned to the others, who quickly confirmed the two likenesses the banker identified.

'Duff Chapter and Gregor Froote,' Essex growled. 'Wanted for armed robbery along the Yellowstone. Looks like they ply their goddamn trade under several aliases too.' Essex shook his head ruefully. 'They looked like a couple o' line workers ... were here all mornin' ... I saw 'em.'

Doc Mulberry gave a thin smile. 'You can't carry a picture of every leery lookin' stranger in your head, Lem,' he said understandingly. 'If I recalled the face of everyone I'd stitched up, there'd be little room for much else.'

'Huh, that's as maybe,' Essex countered uncertainly. 'It don't alter the fact that a good man got himself killed and there's upwards o' five thousand honest dollars gone. I'll send some wires, then go after 'em.'

Through the telegraph agent, he wired news of the robbery, and names and descriptions of the wanted men, to peace officers along the Idaho border. Then he went to enlist the help of Bear Ass Skinner, a man well beyond his three score years and ten, but who had been a celebrated tracker in his time – the time of Christopher Columbus, some townsfolk were often heard to kid.

Though the wind had been spoiling the posse's trail, Skinner was able to follow it easily enough, and an hour's riding brought them to a small desert ranch at Fishtrap's Lake. They learned that Harber Gemm and his posse had stopped there briefly, mentioned they were having trouble pursuing the bank robbers.

It was first dark when Essex and Skinner overhauled the posse riders. They were several miles south of the ranch, and Skinner told them there was no point continuing the search until morning. The sheriff thanked Gemm and his worthy riders, but sent them back to Pony Flats. Weary and disheartened from their fruitless errand, he and Skinner backtracked to spend the night at the Fishtrap ranch.

Another two whole days passed before the sheriff and Skinner returned to Pony Flats. They had scoured the country from the Bitterroot River in the west, to the foothills of the Big Belts in the east. Even to Bear Ass Skinner, it looked like Duff Chapter and Gregor Froote had disappeared into thin air. Lemuel Essex's belief was that the bank robbers had cut back to the rail line and grabbed a freight car heading up to Missoula. He said, 'Maybe there'll be a wire from some border lawman, tellin' me that they've both been taken into custody?' he suggested tentatively.

Skinner coughed and sniggered as he spoke. 'Yeah, when cows climb trees.'

But there *were* communications from one or two border law offices – self-interested requests for more information. Essex was tired and dishevelled, but he wasted no time in returning to the bank.

Wallace Broome was in conversation with someone whom Essex hadn't seen before. 'Any luck, or was it a goose chase?' he asked, with a touch of what sounded curiously like sarcasm.

The sheriff shook his head, carefully eyed the stranger. 'No, none,' he said. 'But I had ol' Bear Ass with me, so it wouldn't have been "luck" if we'd caught up with 'em.'

Broome sniffed tetchily and turned to the man at his desk. 'This is Rufus Maise. He's come out from Helena,' he explained. 'He represents the bonding company that insures the bank – my bank – against robbery, and the like.'

'Well, ain't you the lucky one,' Essex snapped. 'I wonder if the Dunstan girls got insurance against their pa gettin' shot to death in *your* bank?'

Maise, a man with little obvious charm, acknowledged the introduction with a jerk of his head. 'We all appreciate what you're feeling, what you've tried to do, Sheriff, and we'll listen to anything you have to say,' he started in an impassive, well-practised manner. 'However, Chapter and Froote are still at large. I'm here because we can bring resources to bear which are beyond yours, like photographic likenesses and a thousand dollars reward for their capture. I'm putting a couple of detectives on the case, too. They're aboard the Butte-bound right now.'

'That's real accommodatin',' Essex said after a moment. 'But a thousand dollars is a lot cheaper than payin' out full compensation. We mustn't confuse you an' your friends with some sort o' goddamn charity, eh Mr Maise? So are we welcomin' a big-time detective agency?' he continued more sourly. 'Pinkerton men?'

'As good as. They've done work for us before ... always give a good account of 'emselves. Clew and Jesse Brannin.'

'Yeah, I've heard of 'em. I knew 'em both when they were runnin' stock thieves out o' the county. Caution an' courage, Judge Kyte called 'em.'

'They've rose through the ranks since those days,' Maise said. 'They've cracked some big cases and one or two heads along the way, an' they don't come low-cost.'

'No, I'll wager. I guess you'll be payin' 'em ten times what I draw in a month. Let's hope you get your money's worth.'

'Money's our authority, Sheriff. We're

going to use what it buys, to harrow the very souls of that murderous scum,' Maise explained. 'If we want to remain in business, we've to look on all bank robberies the same, no matter how big or small the spoils. If we let them get away with five thousand dollars, next time it might be fifty thousand. Premiums won't cover those losses. I can see that what we're doin' has got you all cross-cut, but there's no reason for you to think we're sidelining you.'

'Maybe that'll be up to the Brannins. An' maybe they'll decide that three's a crowd,' Essex said, getting more irritated at his position. 'Reckon I'll just play my own cards on this one.'

'That's an unfortunate line, Sheriff,' Wallace Broome declared huffily. 'I'd have thought you'd be pleased to have a couple of able men to work with. Let's face it, if *they'd* been in town that morning, Chapter and Froote might be behind bars, right now.'

'I was waitin' for that,' Essex said. His jaw was grinding and his heavy breathing signed his anger. 'Maybe you'd have your goddamn money, but Dunstan would be just as dead.'

'The folk who voted you into your job got a right to expect you to be in town when you're needed – not ten miles away, serving papers over some trivial water rights dispute,' Broome persisted.

'Goddamn you, Broome,' Essex snarled dangerously. 'I would've been here, if I'd got me some help. For years I been askin' for a deputy. "Can't afford it", you bleated, you an' your goddamn cost-cuttin' county officers. So don't blame me for the price you've paid.' Essex lashed out at a spoke chair, kicked it crashing against the dividing counter. Broome grimaced, suddenly nervous of the sheriff's built-up anger. 'There's just one thing more,' Essex continued. 'You've got yourself a sawed-off shotgun under the counter. Why didn't you use it? I would've done, if it had been *my* bank. No, you forget about pannin' me, Broome. There's goin' to be a few folk wonderin' about your efforts long after they've forgotten about mine.'

Maise turned a puzzled look on Broome as the sheriff stormed from the bank. 'There seems to be some internal wrangling he's real torn up about,' he speculated.

'Not exactly the level head we need to help us get this trouble sorted,' Broome replied. 'I'm thinking Lemuel Essex's days as sheriff of Pony Flats are numbered.'

'Well, that's a matter for you and the town. But I wouldn't advise right now,' Maise said pointedly. 'The Brannins might think that every little helps. So, I'll go and see the good Sheriff Essex after he's had time to cool off. With what those outlaws are costing the company, we eat crow if we have to. And that does include you, Mr Broome.'

3

Most law enforcement officers and agencies west of the Missouri and Bighorn rivers had known for some years that Clew and Jesse Brannin were a significant team of man hunters, that their uncompromising capability was matched by their financial reward. But their fellow passengers aboard the Oregon-bound flyer were none the wiser, failed to recognize the tall, dark-featured men who held their own counsel as the miles ticked by.

At Garrison, Clew Brannin had bought a newspaper with a fuller account of the bank robbery at Pony Flats. Prior to that, their knowledge of the robbery had been limited to what they'd learned from Rufus Maise's telegram. After reading no more than half a column, Jesse was of the opinion that rounding up a pair of minor bank robbers wouldn't gain them much in the way of profit *or* interest.

'We shoulda stayed in Bozeman. Chances are, we'll lose a big piece o' work in takin' this on,' he persisted as they neared Pony Flats. 'We should be lookin' east. That's where the real money's movin' around. Real percentage fees for real detectin'.'

'I'm sure you're right, Jesse. But when we started up, *an'* when we most needed it, Maise's bondin' company gave us a lot of work,' Clew said, 'We owe him somethin', so we're goin' on. Besides, we get to renew an old acquaintance. It was Duff Chapter we fingered in that Brewster Store holdup. He got put in the Fort Hogback Pen for five years, so he hasn't wasted much time. Does this other one – Gregor Froote – mean anythin' to you?'

'Never heard of 'im,' Jesse muttered. 'Likely he's out o' the Hogback too.' Jesse took another look at the pictured likeness of Froote. 'His eyes are set close,' he remarked. 'Had me a rabbit like that once. Pa said he was a mean 'un.' Jesse shook his head. 'Robbery an' murder eh? I suppose the dodgers that Maise's bondin' company's sent out say

24

these men are armed an' dangerous an' will resist arrest.'

Clew smiled. 'Well, two out o' three ain't bad.'

The brakeman put his head in at the rear door of the smoker. They were aboard the two-coach evening train that forked west from Garrison to the Butte City spur line. 'Pony Flats,' he yelled. 'Next station Pony Flats. If you're alightin', check your baggages an' traps go with you.'

Clew pulled a clam-sized, silver stem-winder from his waistcoat pocket. 'On time,' he said, and eased himself from his seat.

The train slowed, and the wheels began to screech and grind gently against their brake blocks. Through a side window, Jesse looked out to run his eye over the group of men and women who were milling on the low platform. 'Look there, Clew, they got up a reception committee,' he said jovially.

'Don't want to disappoint you, Jesse,' Clew responded, 'but I reckon there'll be one o' them for almost anythin' that pulls into this one-horse town.'

The sheriff was standing outside of the ticket office, and Clew nudged his brother.

'There's Essex,' he said. 'I heard he was wearin' a badge in this neck o' the woods.'

25

'You reckon he'll remember us?' Jesse asked.

'Yeah. But he won't be glad to see us. We go back some, an' pride's a funny thing with these ol' time law officers,' Clew said, but he wasn't too disturbed.

'You mean knowin' us when we had our asses hangin' from our britches?'

'Yeah, but times change. Let's hope he's gone along with 'em.' Clew shrugged, had a look to check that their range duds, rifles and saddles were ready to offload from the train.

The sheriff recognized the Brannins as they stepped down from their coach, raised his chin in a jerky, uncertain greeting. Rufus Maise assured him that nothing would be done without his knowledge and approval, not unless it was out of his jurisdiction. Interestingly, and more importantly, gave his word that Essex's co-operation would be well rewarded.

'Been a long spell since I last saw you boys,' he said. 'I been hearin' about you from time to time – nothin' that made the funny pages, though. You sure done some growin', Jesse.'

Clew's younger brother gestured a greeting. 'Yeah. I can just about best ol' Clewton with most stuff now.'

26

'Huh, anythin' except work, that is,' Clew said, with a friendly grin. 'Any that comes along when we might have to ride further than the end o' some main street, he wants me to turn it down. Looks like the years ain't been too unkind to you, Lem.'

'Yeah, when the sun's right behind me,' Essex accepted considerately. 'Reckon that's your traps that's bein' stacked up. You bringin' 'em along with us?'

'No. We'll pick it up later, when we have need,' Clew said. 'You ain't got Maise with you then?'

'He's still on bank business ... said he'd come down to my office as soon as he got through. It must be very demandin' work addin' up Broome's new premiums,' Essex said with a fleeting sneer.

'So, how'd you feel towards us lendin' you a hand?' Clew snapped out. 'Don't benefit no one to keep things bottled up.'

'Huh, don't benefit *you,* you mean. Must admit, it did kind o' get me proddy when I heard they'd brought you boys in,' Essex admitted. 'I hardly started off ahead o' the game, an' the goddamn banker ain't lettin' it rest.'

'Ain't lettin' *what* rest?' Jesse asked.

'On the day o' the robbery, Froote an'

Chapter spent all mornin' lollygaggin' in front o' the bank. I saw 'em ... never guessed they were goin' to rob the goddamn place. I even rode out for a few hours.'

'Oh, right. I can see how that must've looked, 'specially to Wallace Broome. But you know what they look like? You went lookin for 'em?' Jesse said.

'Same afternoon ... been out ever since. I had a good tracker with me, too. We didn't get back till a few hours ago. It's been blowin' like hell for a couple o' days, but we managed to stay with 'em till their trail broke up. We couldn't figure how, but it did.'

'I trust you didn't pay the tracker, Lem. Did you get to figure which way they was headed?' Clew asked.

'Yeah, south for nearly twenty miles. Then they struck off towards Gibsonville. Trail went for another ten miles or more, that's when we lost 'em ... still headin' west.'

'Well, it wouldn't have stayed that way for much longer,' Jesse said confidently.

'Hmm,' Essex mused 'Maise said it might end up with you goin' in one direction an' me in another.'

Clew nodded. 'The man's right. That's why we need your help. Stands to reason with us comin' in cold. Suppose you take us to where you're workin' from, Lem. We can get our bearin's, sit down an' talk things through.'

4

Essex led the way along the Pony Flats main street, and in their practised way, the Brannins took in most of the sights and sounds of the town. The sheriff's office was the front half of the county jail and, apart from one homely touch, was as purposeful and cheerless as any other they'd known. A large, romantically coloured print of the Yosemite Valley was pinned to the rear wall of the building and faced the double cell.

'It's for the customers' benefit,' Essex said, when he saw Clew's interest. 'Makes 'em sort o' penitent ... think about what's missin' from their lives.'

'Interestin'. Almost deservin' o' praise,' Jesse mumbled.

Essex pulled a map from the wide drawer of his desk. He opened and spread it across the assortment of leaflets and papers. With his finger, he traced the route he and Bear

Ass Skinner had taken. 'Here's where they turned off to the west,' he said. 'This is mostly broken country, pretty enough, but don't hold too much. If they swung back anywhere else, they took their time doin' it. We rode for miles lookin' for the start o' fresh tracks.'

'They would've ridden that western trail till they thought you'd give up ... and then ridden some more. But they would've turned back south eventually,' Jesse cut in.

'What towns are down that way?' Clew asked.

'A couple o' places that don't show on this map,' Essex told him. 'No more'n scrapes in the dirt. A store maybe, nothin' more. It's tough country, unforgivin' if you don't know it.'

The men sat in the sheriff's assortment of chairs, and discussed options and possibilities.

'Whichever way it cuts, we've got a cold trail to pick up. So we rule out everythin' but what we know,' Clew said.

'What's so wrong with speculation?' Essex wanted to know. 'We're most likely goin' to miss 'em anyway.'

Jesse laughed. 'We got the makin's of a great new force,' he said.

Clew's eyes narrowed in thought. 'We can certainly forget about them makin' north for the railroad,' he advised. 'It's pretty busy up there. Besides, their mounts would've turned up.'

'Not if they'd shot an' left 'em in some high-grassed gully,' the sheriff suggested.

The Brannins gave him a bemused look, didn't respond to the unlikely and disturbing suggestion.

'You've alerted the border law, so it's not likely they'll show anywhere *there*,' Clewton said after a moment. 'An' there's telegraph lines for 'em to stay clear of.'

'I reckon they've been taken in by somebody,' Jesse added.

'Taken in?' Essex repeated doubtfully. 'You reckonin' on three of 'em now?'

'Not necessarily, an' not willingly. But if they ain't got grub, they could resort to some sort o' force. That's what they seem to do if they want somethin'.'

'Yeah, like money. I'll buy that.' Clew looked to Essex who nodded.

'Considerin' what they've done, they'll feel safer if they put a lot o' miles behind 'em. An' they've got money to spend now. They'll want to get on with the spendin' of it.'

'Get on where?' Essex wondered.

'Any of half-a-dozen minin' towns down near the Snake Plain,' Clew said. 'They're boomin' right now – got more wickedness an' back-slidin' than could ever slake a normal man's appetite.'

Jesse rolled his eyes. 'Where'd you recommend we start?' he wanted to know.

'There's a place at the south end o' Bannock Pass, called Whisper. It's as good a place as any.' Essex looked to Clew. 'So, when do we make our move?' he asked.

'If it's all right with you, Lem, we'll light out tomorrow mornin'. We'll ride straight for Jackson Ford ... hole up there for a few days.'

'This side o' the border?'

Clew smiled. 'Yeah. If I'm right, that's the way they'll go. If we get there ahead of 'em, we could bottle 'em up good.'

It was the copper and silver ore that was mined from Beaver Creek that kept the town of Jackson Ford going. For years there had been talk of building a spur line to bring investment for the mines. But it was still in the talking stage, and Jackson Ford's only contact with the outside world remained a twice-weekly stagecoach and a monthly freight team. Clew Brannin was guessing that word of the robbery wouldn't have yet reached there, something that wouldn't have escaped the thinking of Froote and Chapter.

'We got horses in the corral good enough to fill them fine-lookin' saddles o' yours,' Essex said. 'If we pull out at first light, we can be in Jackson Ford late tomorrow night. I hope you both got some food on the train, 'cause my allowances don't run to more'n huck biscuits an' coffee.'

'Yeah, we caught the dinin'-car service between Helena an' Garrison. Wouldn't normally o' bothered, but Maise picks up our expenses.'

Rufus Maise came in as the men sipped the sheriff's coffee. 'I'm glad you were able to get here so quickly,' he said, shaking hands with Clew and Jesse. 'This robbery is like something out of a Ned Buntline dime novel. I trust the three of you have managed to work something out?'

Essex nodded supportively as Clew Brannin explained what they proposed doing.

'Sounds all right to me,' Maise said. 'I'm leaving everything up to you. If you have to get in touch with me for any reason, wire me in Helena. Are you going to the bank to hear Broome's take on it?'

'I know what bank managers have to say,' Jesse said. 'It's usually, no.'

'Yeah, we'll go,' Clew replied. 'The man

ain't goin' to contribute much to what we know, but we don't want any misunderstandin's.' With that, he turned to the sheriff. 'I don't propose to discuss our intentions with him, Lem. But it's his bank, an' as far as I'm concerned, he takes responsibility for its monies. So why not come with me?'

Essex shook his head in clear refusal. 'No. You can tell Broome that if there's anythin' he wants to say to me, he can come here with it. In fact, he can come here an' tell me he's actin' deputy while I'm gone. Besides, I ain't finished my coffee.'

It was usually one of Clew Brannin's procedures to get the main participants involved, but, as he anticipated, nothing came of their discussion with the banker.

'I'm far more interested in seeing those men captured and brought to justice for killing Edgar Dunstan, than for robbing my bank,' Broome said, as Clew and Jesse were leaving. 'I know you Brannins are specialists in your field, so you'll have a plan?'

'Yeah, to go after 'em,' Jesse said sharply, his dislike for the man, obvious.

5

Together with Lemuel Essex, the Brannins rode from Pony Flats shortly after first light. At the tail end of a blue norther, they passed the Fishtrap ranch to find themselves on a grass-covered plain that rolled out before them in never-ending featureless miles.

Regarding the stamina of their grain-fed mounts, they held to a steady comfortable lope, and when they pulled up at noon, they'd not put more than thirty miles behind them. Breaking the horizon to the south, mountains reared their snow-capped backbone.

'The Beaverheads,' Essex pointed out. 'Or maybe you boys don't need me tellin' you that.'

Clew nodded. 'Whatever you think to tell us, Lem. It's been a few years since we last saw 'em. But as I recall, this country's goin' to change some, before we hit Jackson Ford.'

'Yeah, well, that ain't sayin' much. It gets sort o' harder as we near the foothills. The land gets more pinched ... less grass.'

'An' how about Jackson Ford? Has it grown any?'

Essex rocked his head from side to side in way of assessment. 'No, not much. They're migrants mostly. Like nearly all the minin' communities, a real ol' hotchpotch o' peoples an' tongues. Ralph Christian runs a general store, we can get the information we want from him. But we better keep movin'. Moon's goin' to be well up before we get there.'

The land changed as Essex said it would. The Beaverheads were looming ever closer, throwing deep, dark shadows as light began to fall.

'There's some sort o' dust cloud over there to the east. The sun's just about got it lit,' Jesse observed.

Essex squinted against the fast-dropping orb of red light. 'That's the road that connects with the rail-head at Butte,' he said. 'Must be the down stage goin' through. We'll save time if we cut over an' follow it in.'

The moon was high before they caught their first glimpse of the twinkling lights at Jackson Ford.

'Night-time's a bit like when it's covered in snow – as good as anywhere else, an' the only time it gets to look invitin',' Essex rumbled cheerlessly.

The township was a bare and basic creation. All the buildings were single-storey, except for Christian's, the Argent Saloon, and a dance hall which hadn't yet stretched to more than its rough, puncheoned floorboards. At one end of the single street were the miners' canvas-topped cabins; at the other, the gambling tents and red-light quarters of the crib girls.

Christian's store was still open, and there was a small group of men gathered on its stoop frontage when Essex and the Brannins tied in their horses.

As they mounted the steps of the front entrance, Ralph Christian came out to meet them. He was brandishing one of the reward notices that Rufus Maise had sent out, and he called for all to hear.

'I told 'em we'd be seem' you, Lem. The stage just got in with the *Butte Examiner*, an' this handbill addressed to me as postmaster. Too bad you didn't get here earlier, though. He was right here in the store.'

'Who was here?' Essex asked with a rising heart rate.

'Chapter. Duff Chapter. He bought cartridges, some tinned grub an' candy. He's sure a man with a sweet tooth. I recognized his picture straight off.'

The group that had been hanging around the store front, moved closer. One of them stepped up to the sheriff. 'That's right,' he said, peering close with his rheumy old eyes. 'It was that feller Duff Chapter, sure enough. I was in the store talking to Ralph, when he comes in. I didn't take my eyes off him for fear o' somethin' bad happenin'. Yessir, Chapter it was.'

'Yeah, I think we've established that,' Essex rasped.

'If you didn't take your eyes off him, you'd'a seen which way he went,' Jesse said.

'I did, that's a fact. He went straight to the Argent. But he weren't in there long ... comes out with a bottle o' their Pass whiskey. He gets on his horse an' heads off south ... never stopped. Reckon his partner was waitin' for him somewhere along the creek.'

'Yeah, I guess you could be right, mister. Every town sure needs someone like you.' Essex didn't attempt to conceal his irritation. He could have been in Jackson Ford two days ago himself, had he so decided.

'Look on the bright side, Sheriff,' Jesse put in. 'We've picked up three days on 'em. We ain't that far behind.'

They moved into the store, and Essex

introduced his partners to Ralph Christian.

'There's men here could do with a little excitement in their lives. Why don't I organize 'em into a posse?' Christian suggested.

'That ain't normally the business we're in, but we'll think on it,' Jesse said not too seriously.

'What did Chapter say, Ralph?' Essex asked the store owner.

'Not much. He said what he wanted, I set it out on the counter, an' he stuffed it all into a saddle pouch. He did ask how far it was to the border.'

'What did you tell him?'

'What it is. Fifteen miles.'

'Was he surprised?' Jesse asked.

'Didn't appear to be. He said it was about what he figured.'

Jesse nodded. 'That's 'cause he knew. Either him or Froote have been here before. He was just checkin' ... wanted to be sure they could slip across the border in a couple of hours.'

'But they won't do it tonight,' Clew broke in. 'There's no need. They'll wait till daylight before they put Montana *an'us* behind 'em. We'll find 'em camped down the creek eight, ten miles.'

Essex realized that those miles would take

them beyond his jurisdiction. 'Well, I'm all for goin' now. Why wait?' he said.

'Why not?' Clew retorted. 'If they keep movin', we've lost 'em anyway. But if they stay at the creek, we can take 'em in daylight. Bullets an' darkness ain't the best workin' companions.'

'Yeah,' Jesse agreed. 'An' the horses are weary. Let's feed an' rest 'em for an hour or so. An' how about *us*? Can *we* get anythin' this time o' night?' he asked. 'I wouldn't mind a bone to gnaw on.'

'Got nothin' as fancy as that, but I'll make some coffee ... set you a plate o' beans an' bacon,' Christian offered. 'I'll get someone lead your horses around to my barn an' take care of 'em.'

Fifteen minutes later, and after two glasses of corn whiskey, Essex was worrying a little less. As they ate, Jesse held up a brown, plump bean on the end of his fork.

'It's a *bean*, Jesse,' Clew said, guessing it was expected of him.

'I can taste what it's *been*, Clew. I'm wonderin' what the hell it is *now*, for Chris'sakes.'

Clew smiled. 'Eat it up, it won't kill you.'

'Do you know this part o' Beaver Creek?' Jesse enquired of Essex.

'I been up an' down an' around it, once or

twice ... wouldn't say I know it.'

'It would help if we had a man who *does*,' Clew said. 'Knowin' where a feller might strike his camp.'

'Ask Beau Wickett to go with you,' Christian said. 'He knows every foot of it. You want I should call him?'

'Who is he?' Jesse asked.

'Mixed-blood, fur trapper. An' he don't pick or take sides.'

Clew smiled. 'Good. That's what *we* get paid for,' he said.

Essex nodded. 'But two teams o' two's better than one team o' three,' he calculated prudently.

'Chapter an' Froote are wanted for murder as well as bank robbery,' Clew warned the trapper a short while later. 'They'll put up a fight.'

Wickett appeared untroubled and expressed it with a slight shrug. 'So, you pay me fifty dollars when I find 'em,' he said without smiling, but in agreement to riding with them along the creek.

'We leave in an hour,' Clew said decisively.

6

The news of Essex arriving with the Brannins swept through Jackson Ford like a nifty evening breeze. When it transpired that one of the men who'd robbed the bank at Pony Flats, had actually done his marketing in the town, many of those who'd been about to settle into a night's domestic business hurried straight to Christian's store. By the time Beau Wickett and the three lawmen were ready to leave, a significant crowd had gathered out front and in the street. A dozen men were offering to ride with the sheriff, and Essex was obliged to address them.

'If you want to help, get your guns and spend the night down at the creek. But nearby, just in case them fellers break back this way. Perhaps you'd like to organize that, Ralph?'

Thirty minutes later, and just outside of town, Clew drew his colleagues to a halt. 'Jesse and me take one side o' the creek, you an' Wickett take the other,' he directed towards Essex. 'It's the only way we can be sure we don't miss 'em. If you see anythin', drop back an' get word to us. Whatever you do, don't try an' close it out yourself. We'll come an' find you if we get a sniff of 'em. Are we good with that, Lem?'

'Yeah, sure, I want that pair alive. Maise does too. If they know this creek at all, they'd know to ford it right here. There's places where it's goin' to run too deep an' fast to cross just anywhere.'

'That's good thinkin', Sheriff,' Jesse agreed. 'An' up to now, they sure seem to know what they're doin'.'

'There's places where the creek elbows out, an' the banks are wooded tight to the water. So how'd you plan to make contact?' Wickett then asked.

'We give you an' Lem a quarter-hour start,' Clew suggested smartly. 'That'll keep us behind you, an' you'll know where to look for us.' The detective then looked again at Essex. 'An' I don't have to tell you, Lem, that Chapter an' Froote will have real nervy trigger fingers. If you see 'em, stay put an' send Wickett back. If I have to get across to you, I'll find a way.'

Essex and Wickett forded the creek and were soon out of sight. Fifteen minutes later, the Brannins began moving along the west bank. Save for the murmuring of the water, the night was very still, and although there was now bright moonlight, the willow brakes held dark and impenetrable shadows.

Jesse was hunched forward in his saddle, but he was fully alert as he searched the darkness around him. Clew was equally vigilant. Several times they came across small grassy meadows that took them to the water's edge, and they saw evidence that men had camped there, but they were barren and cold sites this night.

Their concentration and the slow, careful pace they pursued started to wear them down. When just an hour had passed, Jesse pulled up and waited for Clew to ride alongside.

'Can't see a goddamn thing, Clew. Could be any sort o' night devil out there.'

'Well if it's Chapter an' Froote, just remember they can't see you.'

'We've come four, maybe five miles?'

'Yeah, I guess,' Clew said. 'It still leaves us time. We ain't lost our retainer yet.'

Midnight was past when a blast of gunshots suddenly fractured the night. They came from further along the creek, but in the pressing disorientation of night, the Brannins couldn't tell how far. And the pattern of shooting told them nothing. It was a full minute more before they heard the sound of pounding hoofs.

'Essex has gone an' jumped 'em, Clew,' Jesse rasped out. 'Goddamn fool didn't wait for us. He saw the promise of a bounty disappearin' across the border.'

Clew was still straining his senses. 'Listen up,' he shooshed. 'That's Wickett. He's ridin' back ... shoutin' for us.'

It took Clew and Jesse a few minutes to find a spot where they could safely ford the creek. They'd only just made it across when Wickett came riding up, breathless and excited.

'They've shot Essex. I reckon they knew we were comin',' he started off at a rate.

'Hey, hold up, Beau. Take it slower,' Clew said, as calm as he was able. 'Just tell us what happened.'

'We moved around a turn in the creek ... was right there, almost on top of 'em. We could see 'em stretched out asleep. Their horses were grazin' beyond the fire. I figured I'd come back for you two ... like we said.'

'What did Essex do?' Jesse asked.

'He said, no. He said, they're where we want 'em, that we should take 'em there.'

'There's a man with conveniently short recall,' Jesse sneered.

'Go on,' Clew urged Wickett to continue.

'We couldn't do much about stayin' upwind, so it woulda been their horses that scented *us* ... probably snickered a bit. Essex charged in, yellin' for 'em to throw up their hands. But them fellers just rolled from their blankets an' started bangin' away like they knew we was comin'.'

'They shot Essex?'

'Yeah, goddamn fool. He took a bullet in the shoulder straight off. They were lyin' doggo ... must've been clutchin' their guns all night.'

'We heard more than one shot,' Clew said.

'The second ... *their* second, knocked him out o' the saddle. I started firin' into the camp, but they'd got me outnumbered ... weren't quite so surprised, I guess. If you heard the shootin' you'll know it was time for me to beat it.

'Yeah, no point in two o' you dyin',' Clew said. 'Essex was distracted, reckless, worried about losin' out on the reward that Maise promised him. He saw a chance to cover himself with glory, too. But you don't win extra pension rights when you're dead.'

'Show us the way back,' Jesse said. 'We'll

go see if there's anythin' left o' this mess to salvage.'

Lemuel Essex wasn't dead. He was conscious when they found him, but bleeding badly from two bullet wounds to his upper body.

'Sorry, boys. I just saw red with them lyin' there, sleepin' like babies.'

Jesse showed little response to finding the sheriff alive. 'Saw your rich pickin's more like,' he ground out.

'Let's see if he'll live,' Clew snapped. 'We can't leave him here, though I'm sorely tempted, goddamnit.'

Jesse toe-poked the ash and dying embers of the fire, asked Wickett to find some blow-down. 'You're a mountain man, ain't you? Get this fire goin',' he said impatiently.

Clew started to cut away Essex's shirt to have a better look at the wounds. 'I guess they're too high to be serious,' he said. 'Not as if they'd holed his bread wallet. What do you usually do with these sort o' wounds?' he asked Wickett who'd got the fire up and burning again.

'Skin it an' roast it, if it was a rabbit or a possum. But for *him*, 'cause he ain't belly shot, I'd give water, tell him he's lucky to be alive. If I was of a forgivin' nature, I'd maybe stuff some wet moss under his vest, for the pain.'

'Is there a doctor in Jackson Ford?'

'Yeah, George Quinnel MD. Most folk who know him, reckon the MD means mules an' dogs. You want me to go for him?'

'Yeah, an' bring a wagon back with you. Can you get through to here?'

Wickett nodded. 'Sure. Got myself a pie buggy ... been haulin' all sorts o' stuff out o' these parts for years.'

'Good,' Clew acknowleged. 'Besides it'll be light by then. You know you got to do your best to keep him alive, Beau.'

'Why *my* best?'

'Because your fifty dollars is within the sheriff's gift,' Clew said with a straight face.

Wickett gave Clew an inscrutable stare, then turned upstream, north, back to Jackson Ford.

'You don't have to carry on with this fussin',' Essex said ungratefully, a few moments later. 'I coulda made it back to town.'

'Yeah, he's right,' Jesse agreed. 'Let's tie the miserable son-of-a-bitch to his horse.'

'You got heartless tendencies, Jesse. You know he'd fall, or bleed to death before he got half the way back. I'll keep an eye on him. Why don't you stretch out for a bit? I'll fetch some o' that moss Wickett was talkin' about an' make up a compress,' Clew said.

'With all them goddamn booger men hidin' in the trees? Thanks, Clew, but I'm stayin' awake.'

'Oh, go to sleep, Jesse, there ain't no more danger here. Chapter an' Froote's goin' to be a lot closer to crossin' that border than they were a couple of hours ago. You can sleep till noon.'

Then Essex spoke. 'Take the horses. Take 'em, an' go after them owlhoots,' he ground out painfully. 'I'll be all right here ... ain't goin' nowhere till Beau gets back with the doc.'

'That's a decent enough thought, an' we could be tempted, Sheriff,' Jesse answered him. 'But me an' my brother are doin' the thinkin' from now on.'

7

'If the sheriff says for you to use his sure-foots, you'd best take him up on it,' Ralph Christian told the Brannins. 'He seems to know his horseflesh, an' he certainly won't be pullin' himself into any saddle for some time to come. Doc says he can't get back to Pony Flats for a week or more.'

It was mid morning, and Jesse and Clew were in Christian's store buying blankets and other cold harbour provisions.

'Ain't quite our normal purchases,' Jesse pointed out to Clew. 'An' when are we supposed to get Essex his mounts back?'

'I don't know. We can always send him a cheque,' Clew answered with a wry smile. 'I want to have a word with Beau Wickett before we pull out, Mr Christian,' he said. 'Can you tell him we'll be in the barn?'

Clew and Jesse were securing the straps of their canvas saddlebags when Wickett joined them.

'I'd like to be goin' with you boys,' he said, 'but I'm thinkin' it would be some time before I'd see Jackson again. An' my life ain't quite through.'

'Yeah, it could be a long an' perilous chase, Beau. You best stick to picnicin' with the coons and bobtails,' Jesse granted. 'But you can still be o' help. Clew wants to ask you somethin'.'

'What's between us an' the border that we got to worry about?' Clew questioned.

'Not a durned thing. Not if you leave the

creek at Bannock Pass.'

'We don't know these places too well. How do we know when we reach the pass?' Jesse asked the trapper.

'Oh, you'll know. There's a place where Beaver Creek makes an ox-bow. Take the bend, then bear south-east. It's a fair climb to the pass, but when you make it, you'll have the Snake Plain ahead o' you. Thirty mile on, an' you'll hit Whisper. I'll wager that's where them two we run into last night are headed.'

'That was my estimation,' Clew said. 'Ain't there a stretch o' rail somewhere down there?'

'There's a few disorganized sections. The Growster-Matches link actually runs into the town ... carries mixed freight. If they get aboard that, they could eventually reach Pocatello an' the Union Pacific.'

'Well, maybe we can head 'em off before then,' Jesse suggested abruptly.

'You'll see one or two cabins, once you're through the pass,' Wickett said. 'You'll be surrounded by the Beaverheads, but that's in your favour. Onto the Plain an' there's only two ways you can get out. Back this way, or head for Whisper. Same for your quarry.'

By mid afternoon, they were into Bannock

Pass. A snow squall struck them and pinned them down for a grim, frosty hour. If there'd been any sign of Duff Chapter and Gregor Froote, it was now long gone.

Jesse sat his horse with his arms wrapped tight. 'We couldn't have missed 'em, so now we know they're ahead of us,' he said with chattering teeth.

'That's about the best of it, Jesse,' Clew agreed. 'With this goddamn snow up here, what's the chances of it rainin' down in the Snake Plain country? It'll slow 'em up, an' they'll keep to the hills an' try to avoid bein' seen. That could give us time to pull ahead of 'em.'

Clear of the pass and the snow, they got hit by belts of heavy rain that slanted in from the east. They were forced to take shelter beneath rocky overhangs, and it shortened their afternoon. It was approaching first dark when they caught sight of a timber hillside lodging. In a pole corral, two forlorn mares stood with their heads close. But there was no sign of any other livestock, and no plough had ever broken the earth that bounded the rudely constructed cabin.

'Looks like the kind o' homestead I'd be keepin',' Jesse said.

'Yeah, I can believe it,' Clew responded. 'I

reckon he's minin'. All wash dirt from those goddamn mountains.'

Jesse pointed at the trail of wood smoke that was being whipped from the pipe chimney. It meant that whoever lived there was at home, and Clew nodded.

They tied their horses to an upright and, as they walked to the cabin, Jesse took a brief look back. A hairy, weather-scoured old man looked them over suspiciously before fully opening the door.

'Ol' timer,' Clew greeted. 'We were passin'.'

'Yeah, I know it. Most o' my guests say that.'

'Your cabin looks real cosy from out there. Mind if we rest up a while?'

'Nope,' the man sniffed. ''Fraid I can't offer you much to drink. I sucked up the last o' my best corn a short while ago.'

'An' *you* probably say *that*,' Jesse muttered under his breath.

An irate-looking wolf-dog tried to force its way out, but the man knee'd him. 'Get back,' he snarled, and gave the animal a boot. It retreated to the fireplace and hunkered down, its jowls, eyes and ears lowered to the hard, dirt-packed floor.

'Fire feels good,' Jesse said, cutting through the cabin's overwhelming ripeness.

53

'There's snow up in the pass.'

'Yeah, I figgered. You on your way down from Jackson Ford?'

'Up an' down, yeah,' Jesse acknowledged. 'My name's Brannin ... Jesse Brannin. This here's my brother Clew.'

'I don't usually go by a name ... no real need. But I'm sometimes Red Hugo,' the old man said, his eyes betraying nothing. 'Why don't you pull them slickers off and dry out? Stay away from where the cur sits, though, he'll tear your ass out, soon as look at you.'

'Where does *he* sit then?' Jesse asked.

'Anywhere he goddamn likes, o' course,' Hugo said, along with a high-pitched snigger.

The Brannins hung their wet oilskins on pegs behind the door, sat either end of a big, flat-topped pine chest.

'Must feel a bit lonesome ... cut-off, up here?' Jesse suggested.

'Yeah,' Hugo replied frankly. 'You're the first fellers I seen in many moons.'

'You could always get down to Whisper, or back to Jackson Ford when you got the leanin',' Jesse continued with a chuckle. He picked up an empty bottle from the floor, took an interested look at the label. 'This must've been the sap you got to weanin' on, eh Red? Too bad me an' Clew are runnin' dry this trip.'

Hugo sniffed his irritation. 'You boys are sure travellin' serious if you ain't got a swig,' he griped. 'You should see the way them city pan washers show up here in the Fall. They want me to guide 'em up in the Beaverheads, with little more'n a comb an' a case of Old Crow.'

Clew nodded courteously. He knew that his brother wasn't that interested, but he wasn't wasting his time either. Jesse was on to something, and Clew would let him play it out, whatever it was.

8

'So you're earnin' a buck by showin' tenderfoots the art o' silver minin', eh?' Clew asked Hugo. 'Not seein' any livestock around, we figured you'd got your own little placer claim.'

'Ha, there ain't no mineral left around here,' Hugo replied. 'Every goddamn square foot's been gone over.' The old man pulled at the wisps of his bedraggled beard. 'Is that the way your toes are pointin?' he asked, giving Jesse and Clew a cunning glance.

'Hell no, we ain't prospectors,' Jesse retorted. 'We got business in Whisper.'

Again, Hugo flicked a wily look at the brothers. 'That'll be some quiet kind o' business then,' he suggested. 'Whisper ain't quite the ol' town she used to be. The last time I was there was late fall, an' there weren't hardly more'n a tent flap movin'.'

'You're gettin' confused, ain't you, Red?' Jesse returned to his concern, exchanged a quick cautionary glance with Clew. 'The label on your whiskey says it came from the Argent saloon in Jackson Ford. So either you been there, an' recently, or we *ain't* the first fellers you seen in many moons. Which is it?'

Hugo hemmed and hawed, scratched the top of his head, let his eyes drift to his rifled musket that was slung above the doorway. 'What the hell's it to you if my bug juice comes from Jackson or Whisper or goddamn China?' he snatched out angrily. His tone aroused the dog who raised its eyes and growled a warning.

'We know where it came *from,* Red, an' we don't care. It's how you got it, that concerns us. An' there's mares in your corral, carryin'

56

brands that don't belong here. You know the penalty for takin' ownership of stolen stock's quite breathtakin' in Montana.'

The Brannins had no evidence that the horses had been stolen, but with their increasing suspicions, it seemed a fair guess they had been.

'Up in these godforsaken parts, me an' Jesse are the next best thing to the law, Red,' Clew put in drily. 'So you just tell us that this carrion was up here this mornin' an' we can all get on with our business.' With that, he pulled out a reward dodger, unfolded it and held it out for Hugo to see. 'Recognize 'em?' he asked.

The old man was considering reaching up for the musket, but Jesse reached out a restraining hand and smiled tolerantly.

'These men ain't only wanted for robbery an' murder in Pony Flats, Red. Last night they shot down the sheriff of Jackson Ford,' Clew continued. 'Under any ol' goddamn law, them's most grave crimes. They figure alongside horse stealin' an' tellin' lies to us. So unless you speak up, ol' man, you'll find there's a big pile o' trouble sittin' your stoop.'

Red Hugo knew it. 'All right,' he said, 'I'll tell you. They *was* here this mornin'. They come in all friendly like, an' then the little one pokes a gun barrel at me while I make them some goddamn breakfast. Then he gets me to fry the dog's goddamn coon livers. It was them that brought the whiskey. They left it on the table with a double eagle for me to keep my mouth shut.'

'They drank a bottle o' double-rectified between 'em, before ridin' off?' Jesse asked in amazement.

'No, that was *my* breakfast,' Hugo owned up.

'When did they show? What time?'

'Early, before seven.'

'They say where they was headed?' Clew asked.

'Nope. But I watched 'em for a while. They was makin' for the plain, it looked like.'

'Well, there's a thousand-dollar reward on their heads, dead or alive. If they show up again, you best remember it,' Clew informed him, satisfied they now had the truth.

'That's a lot o' needful, an' I could sure use it,' the old man said thoughtfully. 'Do I get to keep the gold piece?'

'Yeah, I guess. You didn't have to mention it. How far before we hit the first o' the cattle ranches?' Clew asked.

'Twenty-five miles, more or less. An' you won't find no trail or road till you get down to the Erskine stock pens. If them two fellers you're after ain't stopped for nothin', they'd have made Whisper by noon. You're a ways behind 'em.'

'But if they ride into town careless, they might just get the attention o' Long John Shallote,' Clew said. 'He was telegraphed to be on the lookout for 'em, soon after they hightailed it from Pony Flats.'

'Is there a night train from Whisper?' Jesse asked.

'Nope. Comes in one mornin', goes out the next. Hurd Growster owns most of it. It's just a string o' wreck wagons. If you want a seat, it'll be on the cow catch.'

'Looks like the rain's eased,' Clew said, as he and Jesse picked up their slickers. 'Be seem' you, ol' timer.'

Hugo's dog barked and leapt for the doorway, but this time he let it run. It raced to the feet of Jesse's horse and looked up quizzically, waited for the command to bite.

'I don't own them mares,' the old miner called out, as Jesse and Clew rode away. 'They said they'd be comin' back for 'em.'

'He's a shifty old rogue,' Jesse remarked, minutes later. 'But he don't gain by goin' windy on us. So we ain't ridin' to Whisper on a notion.'

'No, they're out there sure enough,' Clew returned. 'I'm concerned at the thought o' John Shallotte lyin' in wait for 'em, though. If he thought Chapter an' Froote were headed his way, he'd be gettin' set to take 'em out himself. An' he's got to be seventy if he's a day.'

Jesse nodded. 'Why'd you mention it ... back there?' he asked.

'In case they turn back. A warnin' from ol' Red might ring herd 'em.'

Jesse let the reckoning sink in. 'It's goin' to be full dark in an hour, Clew,' he then said. 'How far you figurin' to go before we roll up the day?'

'We can pull in now if you want, but I think we should go on. We can make up some time ... be in Whisper before midnight.'

'What do we gain from that?' Jesse doubted. 'You heard that Whisper ain't no hell on wheels any more. If Long John Shallote ain't got the teeth he used to, he'll damn sure have the town locked up tight as a tick afore he goes to bed.'

Clew turned in his saddle and gave Jesse a long look. 'We missed 'em at Jackson Ford by a few hours, an' then 'cause of Essex's play, again last night. We're both plumb tired, Jesse, but we ain't gettin' paid to miss 'em a third time, an' you know it.'

'Goddamnit, Clew, it ain't *me* that's wantin' a rest. These mounts got foldin' necks an' legs,' Jesse snapped. 'It must be a hundred miles from Pony Flats to Whisper, an' that's too much in forty hours. We've even clambered up an' down a mountain since Jackson Ford. We'll find us some cover an' rest up for a few hours, as long as we're in town before that train pulls out in the mornin'.'

From Jesse's abrupt manner, it was plain to Clew that his brother was as weary as the horses – they both were. 'Yeah, you're right,' he said. 'I just wondered how it stacked up with you.'

9

Whisper's main street was deserted when Clew and Jesse rode in.

'Reckon our friend Red was right,' Jesse said, eyeing a pair of empty buildings, the boarded-up windows.

'Yeah, a town livin' down to its name,' Clew agreed. 'Still, any point with a train that calls in, ain't quite dead. Essex reckoned there's still just about one of everythin'. Let's ride down to the depot.'

The Growster-Matches Link train consisted of a passenger-caboose and three flatcars. The funnel-stacked engine stood hissing on the track, as the fireman kept a gradual head of steam.

'What time you pullin' out?' Clew hailed.

The fireman looked at Clew and Jesse carefully. 'When we can't get any more on board. Another hour, maybe,' he said, coolly.

Clew returned the man's appraising look. 'Is there anyone makes food in this town?' he asked.

'You'd have come by a pile o' cedar logs, when you rode in. If you'd looked close, you'd've seen a sign. It's Rowan's Hotel. Try there.'

'We will.' Clew thanked him and, with Jesse, turned back up the street.

'He sure gave us a good lookin' over,' Jesse said.

Clew nodded, 'Yeah, I noticed. John Shallote's obviously passed the word to be on the lookout for strangers.'

HARDLY EVER CLOSED the plain painted notice said. The low building stood sideways on to the road, looked more like a sod house claim than a hotel.

They tied their horses securely to the runners of an upturned mud boat. 'Ain't rightly ours to take chances with,' Jesse pointed out.

'Would you boys like a table?' Rowan Vine asked, almost as soon as Clew pushed against the log door.

'Long's it ain't in front of a saddle,' Clew answered pleasantly.

The girl's green eyes closely examined Clew and Jesse as she gave details of the food on offer.

'For goodness sake, missy, we look nothin' like 'em,' Clew said, retaining a smile.

'Look like *who?*' the girl asked.

'Them bank robbers whose pictures you're confusin' us with.'

'No, I'm not. But only 'cause now I've had me a good look,' she answered back. 'A girl wouldn't want to put either o' *their* pictures on her wall,' she added cheekily.

Jesse laughed. 'Why don't you bring me some tinned milk an' peaches, with the ham an' egg, I'm needin'? If you got coffee ready, you can bring that too.'

'Sounds good. Me as well,' Clew said. 'So what time o' the mornin' does Sheriff Shallote go by?'

'It varies. But this mornin' I'd say he ain't too far away,' she replied. She took a step to the side loophole window and ducked her head to look up the street. 'Yep, he's comin'.'

A moment later, Whisper's long-time sheriff stood in the doorway. John Shallote was a lean, hard-looking man with long grey hair, and he carried a conspicuous single-barrel shotgun in his left hand. He levelled a bright glance at the Brannins, and a stiff grin broke his tough features.

'Come right on in,' Clew hailed him. 'Don't stand there on ceremony in your own town.'

'I don't often get surprised at this time o' day, but it sure weren't you two I was expectin'. Otherwise, I'd have left this ol' firestick at home,' Shallote replied. He stepped up to the table and offered his hand to Clew then Jesse.

'The years at Whisper have been kind to you, John,' Clew said affably.

'Yeah, most of 'em,' Shallote replied. Then the thought hit him. 'You're goin' to tell me it's the bank robbery at Pony Flats that's brought you down here.'

Clew nodded and grinned. 'Left yesterday at noon came over the pass from Jackson Ford. You seem to have got most folk around here on the lookout, John.'

'In this business, no one gets to my age without some farsightedness,' Shallote said.

'After I got a wire from Lemuel Essex, I got to thinkin' that if it was *me* did the robbin' an' killin', I'd be headed south. But I can tell you for a fact that they ain't yet gone through here. How do you boys know they're headed this way?'

'Because we missed 'em by a few hours at Jackson Ford, an' again a few hours later along Beaver Creek,' Jesse contributed.

'Since yesterday mornin' they've been out on the Snake Plain,' Clew added. 'Sit yourself down for a while.'

'I'll take some coffee. Can't fit much atop a "Long John" breakfast.'

Jesse thought for a moment, then went into the yarn with a wry smile. 'What's a "Long John" breakfast?' he asked.

'A two pound buffler steak, a bottle o' good forty-rod an' the use o' Rowan Vine's dog.'

'What's the dog for?' Clew joined in, taking the bait.

'Eatin' the goddamn steak, o' course.' The three men laughed, and Shallote followed up on his earlier query. 'So you picked up their trail after you came over the pass?'

'Sort of. You know Red Hugo's cabin?' Clew asked him.

'Only to stay clear of it. Some days you can smell it from here. They were there?'

'Yeah. They stopped to swap horses.' Clew saw no point in mentioning anything else.

'Hmm. Have they any reason to believe you boys are chasin' 'em?'

'Not *us,* no. But they'd surely guess that somebody would be. Are you wonderin' why they didn't ride into town yesterday?'

John Shallote shrugged. 'It did cross my mind. Maybe they wanted time to think, I don't know. But if they don't show this mornin', we'll have to give it some thought. When you've eaten, we'll take a walk. I'll ask Rowan about gettin' your mounts taken care of.'

Thirty minutes later, the three men were standing on the low jetty of Whisper's rail depot.

'If we get into a gun fight, I hope I don't get belly shot. Sure be a waste o' them good fixin's,' Jesse said in black humour.

John Shallote acknowledged the engineer and the fireman. The tallyman stepped down from the rear of the caboose, the last of the train's four wagons. 'Mornin', Sheriff,' he shouted. 'No passengers, an' the freight's loaded. Train can leave anytime,' he shouted.

'We'll give it a few more minutes,' Shallote said, glancing at his watch. 'If they show up, we'll let 'em get aboard before we make a move. You boys take the rear steps.'

'Your town, your play, John,' Clew agreed. 'But just be sure *we're* in there, before you do anythin'. We don't want another sheriff goin' for glory.'

'Where does this train pull to, after here?' Jesse asked.

'Assumin' it ain't goin' up to the Peak, *nowhere,* until it gets to Pocatello. Not unless someone stops it, o' course. But I warned 'em on the footplate that if Chapter an' Froote flag the train, they're to leave 'em standin'. Mind you, with the load o' plunder this gal's puffin', you could walk faster.'

Clew looked the engine over – its leaky steam box, rusted paint and tarnished brass-work. 'Like us, eh John ... seen better days? Red Hugo told us the company's in trouble.'

'Yeah, so much so it's up for auction. When Hurd Growster's taken the last o' the building timbers, he'll start on the iron an' ties. He'll probably salvage 'em as his last train pulls out. Can't really blame him for stealin' a dyin' town.'

Jesse had walked the length of the train, looked at the loads of stacked lumber, glanced under the cars, making sure no one was riding the rods.

Soon, the tallyman was shouting for people

to board the train, almost as though he believed there might be some last-minute passengers. With a cough and a spit of power the drivewheels started to take hold. The engineer gave a satisfied look down at the sheriff, let some steam into the engine's whistle.

'No sign, goddamnit,' Shallote muttered. 'They're goin' to ride across the Beaverheads, an' board at some other stop clear o' the border. We've lost 'em, boys.'

Clew didn't move a muscle, kept his eyes on the sheriff. 'Don't get too excited, ol' feller, but we ain't lost 'em. They're here, an' gettin' set to board.'

10

The train had picked up a little speed when Duff Chapter and Gregor Froote appeared from the blind side of a wayside cabin. The engineer still had his hand on the whistle cord, when Chapter grabbed the hand rail and swung up into his cab. The fireman had been looking from the off-side window, and before they knew what was happening, Chapter had them covered. Froote climbed in after him, flung his saddle-bags across the floor of the cab and pulled his own Colt.

Jesse ran for the last flatcar and grabbed at a corner stanchion. Clew was close behind him, reaching for a rail at the rear of the caboose. As soon as his feet found the step, he pulled himself onto the iron platform. Long John Shallote, for all his vim, was left behind.

Clew looked back for a brief moment. 'That's somethin' else about bein' seventy,' he muttered. Then, checking the empty bunks, he ran through the decrepit caboose to reach Jesse.

'We'll have to scramble over this lot,' Jesse said, when Clew got to him. 'An' before they cut the goddamn engine away from us.'

Clew shook his head. 'They don't know we're here.'

'To rid 'emselves o' the load. Must be ten tons of old lumber on these cars,' Jesse reasoned. 'Keep low, an' we'll get to 'em easy enough.'

Clew and Jesse bent double as they made their way forward. The train was moving faster, but it wasn't too difficult treading through the mixed timber and across the securing chains. They quickly reached the tender that was stacked with lumps of cordwood, crept flat out with their heads below the skyline, away from the bank robbers' sight. Below them, Chapter had the engineer covered, and Gregor Froote was doing likewise with the fireman.

Jesse indicated that they inch forward, but the train jolted over a loose section and Clew's foot dislodged a wedge of firewood. Chapter half turned, saw Clew and fired simultaneously. The bullet ploughed the top of Clew's outstretched left arm, clipped his shoulder, and thumped past his jawbone.

As Clew backed off, Chapter dropped to his knees and began shooting wildly up across the top of the cordwood pile. Jesse swore and raised himself, his lower legs clamped to the end of a tie-beam. He took a two-handed aim and loosed off a single shot down at Chapter. The man yelled, threw up his gun, and fell.

Froote was hunched in the opposite corner to where Chapter was writhing on the floor of the engine cab. He reached for Chapter's dropped Colt, levelled both his guns up at where he thought Clew or Jesse would next show themselves.

Clew kicked out at the cordwood, sent half a dozen or more crashing down into the cab. Froote defended himself, but before he could retaliate with gunfire, the fireman

70

grabbed his long-handled stoker and swung it into the side of Froote's head. The short, tight-featured man grunted, went down as the stomach-churning noise filled the confines of the steamy cab.

Clew cursed at the brutality of the move. 'You got the makin's of goddamn fine sheriff, mister,' he yelled.

The engineer made a grab for the throttle lever with his left hand, and spun the brake wheel with his right. As the train slowed, Chapter rolled onto his side. He got to his knees, then pushed himself out through the cab's doorway. He landed tight beside the track, but before he could think about getting anywhere, he took a pounding kick in the ribs, then another in the back of his neck.

'That's for shootin' up my arm, Chapter. Now crawl, you murderous scum,' Clew rasped.

The tallyman started running from the depot as soon as the train stopped. 'Heard the shootin',' he puffed excitedly. 'You got 'em both? Where's the other one?'

'In the cab. Get this one back on his feet, an' on board. Kick him again if you have to. It was your train he was stealin',' Clew directed Hurd Growster's tallyman.

'I got one here who ain't goin' anywhere

71

under his own steam,' Jesse grinned roguishly, as he leaned out from the cab. 'You want we should back up to the depot?'

'Yeah, give us as minute, an' grab the saddle-bags,' Clew shouted back. He indicated to the tallyman that Chapter should be forced up onto the bed of the first flatcar. 'Comfort ain't a concern,' he said scornfully.

As the train backed slowly to the Whisper depot, Chapter looked up from where he was slumped. 'Where in hell's name did you come from, Brannin?' he snarled meanly. 'Seems a man can't draw cash, without you an' that brother o' yours showin' up.'

'You must've heard that times are changin', Chapter,' Clew said. 'Well, these are them.'

'Not yet,' Chapter retaliated, painfully defiant.

'You're the one with a big Colt threatenin' the front his face. An' it ain't just about unlawful bankin'. You shot a man dead in Pony Flats.'

Chapter's impassive eyes focused on Clew's blood-soaked sleeve. 'I warned him, told him not to try anythin' stupid. The half-bake must've had some goddamn death wish.'

11

News of the capture of the killer bank robbers spread quickly, and more than a fair share of Whisper's dwindling population turned out to see Chapter and Froote taken up the main street. Chapter was forced to walk, but Froote had to be carried in a makeshift stretcher. When the pair were under lock and key, John Shallote sat with the Brannins in his office.

'Weren't much help to you boys,' he said ruefully. 'Like as not, I'd have broke my neck, if I'd had to grab for anythin' on that train.'

'Possibly. But you'd already done your bit, John,' Clew told him. 'Chapter was in town last evenin', an' it seems they did plan to flag the train between here an' the border. It was only 'cause o' your warnin' the crew, that put 'em off the idea. We wouldn't have either of 'em locked up if it weren't for your use o' brain over brawn.'

'Yeah, an' there'll be some reward money comin',' Jesse added, bearing in mind that nearly all the money stolen from the Pony

73

Flats bank was found in Gregor Froote's saddle-bags.

'We'll deposit it all at the miners' bank, then get you over to Tom Kelso's surgery,' Shallote said. 'Jesse, if you wouldn't mind waitin' here? Tell these birds that if either of 'em starts squawkin' about their wounds, or anythin', I'll have the doc take the scenic route to get here. Take a look through the reward dodgers, why don't you? Maybe there's a new dollar or two to be made.'

They were gone an hour, and when they returned, Clew was supporting his injured arm in a muslin sling.

'The doc says, I got to keep it this way for two or three days,' Clew responded to Jesse's incredulous look. 'If I don't, it'll maybe take two or three weeks.'

'Keep it in the goddamn sling,' Jesse muttered. Then he turned to Shallote. 'Are you stayin'?'

'Yeah, until Doc Kelso gets here,' the sheriff replied. 'If I need a deputy, I can swear in Butch Harries. How long do you figure it'll be before somebody gets sent to collect 'em?'

'Don't know or care that much,' Clew said. 'As long as they don't get loose, our job's finished. If you can get Essex his horses back, an' if that train's makin' just one more trip, we'll buy a ride. From Butte City we can get to Garrison, then Bozeman.'

'Meantime we'll have your depot's telegraph office send our wires,' Jesse.

As they approached the rail depot, Jesse saw that its lean-to office wasn't being manned by the line's tally man.

'I'm Jesse Brannin, an' this here's Clew Brannin,' Jesse informed the slim, raven-haired girl behind the desk. 'We got some wires to send.'

'Yeah, I know who you are. I'm Milly Matches, an' there's telegraph blanks on the desk if you come on in,' the girl said, lifting a long draw-bolt.

'This your part o' the business?' Clew asked as he stepped into an office decorated with yellow and white sheets of bygone haulage transactions.

'Yeah, but it don't look like for much longer. When your takin's are down to a dollar a day, it ain't much more'n name only.'

'I'm sorry about the delayed train,' Clew apologized.

'That's all right. It ain't really for passengers. Most folk are surprised it's there at all.'

'Yeah, I heard,' Clew said. He picked up a pencil stub and wrote telegrams to Rufus Maise in Helena, and Lemuel Essex in Pony

Flats. 'So, what happens to you, Milly Matches, when you do close?' he asked.

'I'm hopin' Hurd Growster will compensate. He owes me somethin'. It's through *my* good office that most of his dealin's are transacted. An' talkin' o' business, what is it o' yours?' she added tartly.

Clew held up his hands. 'None,' he said with a weak smile. 'But, single-handedly, I've just equalled your day's takin's. Perhaps things are on the up.'

Milly tried the smile back, but it didn't work.

'Can't some o' the ranches on Snake Plain use rail track to get their beef to Pocatello?' Clew continued. 'Ain't many of 'em from what we saw, but it would sure be convenient ... enough to support the line with you an' your business.'

'Instead of runnin' 'em across to the Challis pens, you mean? Yeah, they could, if they hadn't been advised not to.'

'Advised not to? Who'd advise 'em that?'

'The bank. Mr Rawfield.'

'Rawfield? The owner o' the Double R ranch?'

Milly nodded. 'Yeah, one an' the same. Austen Rawfield.'

'Well, that don't make much sense. He

must know somethin' you all don't.' Clew turned to involve Jesse who'd been listening with interest.

'Or maybe somethin' that you *do* know. But cattle, or salvage, or any other kind o' business don't figure,' Jesse hinted.

The suggestion was unexpected. Milly was suddenly a little agitated, and she coloured up. 'Look, it's all too late now, an' I'd–'

'Sorry, ma'am, this really ain't none of our business,' Clew chipped in. 'It's just that in our line o' work, we're always gettin' to hear o' curious, doubtful deals. Sometimes, it troubles us.'

Clew paid Milly for the telegrams. 'We'll come by later in the day. See if there's any response.'

'You'll be stoppin' at Rowan's?' she said, perking up. 'It is the best place in town.'

'It's the *only* place we were told. A town with one of everythin'.'

The two men had hardly cleared the depot's yard, when Clew rounded on Jesse. 'What the hell did you mean, suggestin' there was somethin' else between Rawfield an' her?' he questioned. 'For Chris'sake's Jesse, if you're *that* interested, ask ol' Long John. He's sure to know.'

'I'm goin' to. Like you say, Clew, sometimes we get troubled. Well, this could be one o' them times.'

'I reckon you gone an' got your head turned by a petticoat, Jesse.'

'Weren't quite that lucky, Clew. But just give it a moment's thought. Why don't the ranchers use the Growster-Matches Link? Losin' all that profitable lard on long drives out to Challis don't make any sense. Goddamnit, they probably get shipped down to Pocatello from there. An' who the hell's this big shot Rawfield?'

Clew gave a perceptive smile. 'Yeah,' he said, 'I think that's the bit that could trouble *me*. Meantime, let's get ourselves boarded.'

Their horses had been watered and fed, were still outside of the Vine Hotel. After booking themselves two of Rowan Vine's three rooms, they walked them down to John Shallote's office.

Doc Kelso had attended to Chapter and Froote, was leaving as they arrived.

'How's Froote?' Jesse asked. 'The last time I saw him, he was havin' an iron bar pulled from the side of his nasty little head.'

'He's lucky to be alive. If it was a skull that carried any grey matter inside it, he surely would be dead. The other one's bruised up an' lost some blood. Regrettably, not lost the instinct for life.'

'You can always leave your saddles in here till you need 'em. If an' when the time comes,' Shallote offered.

'Thanks, John. I'm just goin' to rest up. I'll sit outside a while on Doc's orders,' Clew said, knowing that Jesse had a question or two for the sheriff.

'It don't make sense to a lot o' folk, what Austen Rawfield's up to,' Shallote said, in answer to Jesse's question. 'But I reckon it's all 'cause of his boy, Brady. There's somethin' between him an' Miss Milly, an' the ol' boy don't like it.'

'Sorry, John, you got me there. You're sayin' that Rawfield's drivin' cattle halfway across the world to Challis, 'cause his boy's sweet on Milly Matches?'

'Yep. An' he figures when the line closes, Milly takes the last train out with Hurd Growster.'

'I can see why this don't make a lot o' sense. I thought the town was goin' cold 'cause the silver's run out. You're sayin' it's since the ranchers have stopped pushin' their beef through?'

'I'm sayin' the train link wouldn't have to close if they did.'

'And Milly Matches would get to stay?'

79

'Yep.'

Jesse swore. 'That's the goddamn stupidest thing I've ever heard, an' I don't believe it. There's somethin' else goin' on, an' I'll wager this young Brady knows what it is.'

Anything else that Jesse was about to get heatedly interested in, was drowned out by a disturbance beyond the wall that divided the cell tier at the back end of the office.

'What the hell's that?' the sheriff yelled. 'Sounds like them goddamn prisoners are tearin' my jail apart.'

Clew rolled sideways from his chair, quickly stepped inside as Shallote was pulling at the iron-strapped connecting door.

Duff Chapter was sitting on his bench palette, swinging a heavy wooden stool against the door of their cell. 'We ain't ate since noon yesterday,' he grated. 'Bring us a platter.'

'You had a choice, an' decided to go for train stealin',' Shallote snapped back angrily.

'You're supposed to feed us,' Chapter shouted fiercely. 'You lettin' us go hungry an' pocketin' the money, you star-totin' son-of-a-bitch?'

Before Shallote could respond, Jesse moved up close to the cell bars. 'You want me to go get that fireman ... him an' his stokin' piece?'

80

he warned menacingly. 'Just ask your quiet friend there what it feels like to get slapped by *that*. Now shut your noise, or you'll get more than a gravy biscuit in your kisser.'

Chapter had shrunk back into an enfeebled silence, and Shallote had just slammed the door closed when a tall man walked confidently into the office. His short-cropped hair was nearly white and he was wearing a dark suit. Jesse and Clew were in no immediate doubt that the man was Austen Rawfield.

'Ah, Austen. I thought you'd be by,' Shallote greeted him. 'Glad, too. These are the two detectives from Helena way, you'll have heard about. It's mostly down to them that we've got Chapter an' Froote in iron lodgin's. They'll have robbed an' killed *their* last.'

'I hope so, John,' Rawfield said. He looked hard at Jesse, then at Clew. 'You got warrants for their arrest?' he asked rudely.

'No,' Clew answered just as abruptly. 'Whoever comes down for 'em will bring those. You got a reason for askin'?'

Rawfield sniffed. 'I was thinkin' that without warrants, Shallote can't hold 'em indefinitely. Not unless he brings some charges against 'em.'

'I can hold 'em two or three days without

doin' that,' Shallote said.

'It's a mighty odd sort o' question to come visitin' with, Mr Rawfield,' Jesse said, the irritation clear in his voice. 'Sounds like you got some sort of authority, makin' some kind o' threat, even.'

'Just get 'em charged. I don't want it hangin' over into Friday. There's an auction, an' I want everythin' cleared by then.'

Clew was about to ask Rawfield what it was to him, what the hell difference it made, when the man turned on his heel. Within a moment he was gone from the office.

'So, that's the big shot Rawfleld?' Jesse said with a flat grin. 'He certainly throws his weight around like he's used to it.'

'Yeah,' Clew agreed. 'So it's Friday when the line goes under the hammer, is it? An' Rawfield ain't interested in the outfit? Huh. Believe that, an' you'll believe anythin'.'

'Well, he's the bank ... the official receiver, so I won't be acceptin' a bid from him,' Shallote observed.

'But you will be, from whoever's there to do his biddin',' Clew said. 'No wonder he ain't done much about Hurd Growster's flatcars. With what's left o' the town, he'll probably get the whole kit an' caboodle for little more than its scrap value.'

Clew then turned tiredly to his brother. 'I reckon that laudanum's gettin' to me, Jesse,' he said. 'Maybe I'll just go along with them two days o' rest. I guess lookin' at Mr Austen Rawfield's real purpose shouldn't be too demandin'. In a way, it's our civic duty.'

'Now listen, fellers,' the sheriff started. 'Rawfield's a respected man in these parts, not some goddamn boodlestiff. He runs the bank, for Chris'sakes. He don't give many breaks, but that's the nature of his business, an' it don't put him outside o' the law. You're goin' to ruffle feathers, you go pokin' your nose into his affairs.'

'We're detectives, Sheriff, an' *that's* the nature of our business,' Jesse concluded wryly.

12

On returning to the depot early afternoon, Milly Matches handed Clew a telegram that had been filed at Helena – a brief, congratulatory message from Rufus Maise. It was followed later by a longer message, asking the brothers to remain in Whisper until the warrants came through. Maise said that he'd been in touch with Lemuel Essex who'd now returned to Pony Flats. A deputy marshal had visited the sheriff, and would be on his way to Whisper after visiting the main Helena office.

Clew handed the message to Jesse. 'I'm surprised he ain't askin' us to sleep in with Chapter an' Froote. That's why he wants us to stay – he figures they might bust away from ol' Long John.'

They didn't attempt to sound out Milly any further on the sale of the line. Clew thought that relevant information wasn't likely to be had from her.

'I'm usually here till six. But I can keep the key open if you want,' she offered. 'Perhaps there'll be somethin' for you later.'

'Thanks, Milly, but you go when you normally do. If there is anythin' after that, we'll collect in the mornin',' Clew said.

A while later, the pair called into Hudson's Mercantile. They were making trivial purchases, and Clew wondered if the proprietor was the customary font of local news and opinion.

'What are you folk goin' to do here? With the line closin' an' all, the town's fit to blow away,' he started off cordially.

'Well, if I have to pull up stakes, I can, an' will. But it won't be just yet,' Enoch Hudson answered, folding up a red linen bandanna.

'Well, if it was my town, I wouldn't want to be forced away,' Clew said. 'I'd try an' persuade Rawfield to think more favourable. Ain't you got a town council? There must be enough o' you general traders an' ranchers left ... a bit o' collective muscle.'

'Huh, we ain't *that* collective. Not any more.' Hudson shook his head. 'Most are just fearful of him. All it took was a note here, an' a mortgage there. I've known him for twenty years, an' never owed him a penny. So, I'm aimin' to stick around to see what he's got in mind for ol' Whisper. The man ain't bankin' a loser, that's for sure.'

'There's always a first time,' Jesse observed snappily.

'No *that* kind o' first, there ain't. Where's his business if Whisper does dry up? He's losin' money already, trailin' his beef to Challis. It needs a big outfit too. No, there's somethin' else, somethin' with a financial edge,' was Hudson's assessment.

'Yeah, maybe you're right. It's been interestin' talkin' to you,' Clew said, as he paid the man.

'What do you think?' Jesse said, when they

85

were back on the street.

'I think he's right. Rawfield's playin' for more than a dilapidated railroad. That's bluff money as far as he's concerned. An' we can't do much for Miss Matches until we know what *real* edge Mr Hudson's talkin' about.'

They were at the depot again shortly after five. A message had arrived from Essex, confirming Maise's statement that a deputy marshal had been and gone from Pony Flats.

'I reckon Lem's flown his bed. He's probably punchin' walls 'cause he weren't in on the capture,' Jesse remarked. 'The fool could've been, if he hadn't charged in so.'

Clew nodded at an old man who was sitting on a bench at the end of the depot's jetty. 'Evenin', ol' timer,' he said. 'Mind if we sit awhile?'

'Nope. Help yourself, I know who you are.'

'Yeah, I guess you do,' Clew said, and eased himself onto the seat. Jesse stood off, looked along the track towards the Beaverheads.

'You sit here long enough, you get to see just about everythin', I guess,' Clew said.

'Yep, you sit here long enough,' the old man agreed impassively.

'So, if there'd been any strangers in town – ones who'd been visitin' Austen Rawfield –

86

you'd most probably know?'

'Yep, most probably. But there ain't. It's the other way round. It's Rawfield that's been out o' town, runnin' up to Butte City.'

'Well, he's a businessman. They've probably got more'n one bank, up there.'

'He ain't one for unnecessary travel, though.'

'Perhaps it weren't on bankin' matters. Has he got any interests in minin'?'

'You ask a lot o' questions, mister,' the old man charged.

'Yeah? Well, if you know who I am, you'll know it's what I do. Ain't too different from you an' your lookin', you nosy ol' goat. Now, tell me about Rawfield's minin' interests.'

The old man considered Clew's response for a moment, then chuckled, dribbled a thin stream of dark juice down between his knees. 'Depends what you mean by "interests". He's put more in than he's taken out, I know that much.' He wiped the back of his hand across his stained moustache, took a more direct look at Clew. 'Funnily enough, I did hear that he's put a couple o' prospect diggers up on Blue Peak. Took a whole load of equipment with 'em, too.'

'What would they be lookin' for, up there?'

'I never heard that. But silver ain't the only

precious metal.'

Just then, Jesse gave a short, sharp whistle. The men looked up, turned round to see a hand car rumbling along the rail track from the northern end of the town.

A tall, raw-boned man was pumping it, and when he reached the depot he pushed the car into the pass junction.

'Where the hell did that come from?' Clew asked.

'The Double R. They got a leased sidin' that runs to their cattle pens. That's Brady Rawfield, an' he's just got to be workin' somethin' from his system.'

'So, the young Lothario? Wasn't it *him* you wanted to have a word with?' he asked of Jesse.

Jesse shook his head. 'It can wait. He couldn't give us much more'n what you been gettin'.'

The Brannins discussed the circumstances as they walked back to the jail. When they arrived, the sheriff was talking to Butch Harries.

'Whatever you gone an' decided,' Jesse cautioned, 'don't go near them cells tonight. Not even to provoke 'em. They're cornered an' they're hurt. Given a chance, they'll fox you, use every sly, goddamn cunnin' trick to get out o' here.'

'They won't put anythin' past me,' Harries assured him.

Clew exchanged a sceptical look with Jesse. 'One of us will drop by later, an' see how you're all doin',' he said.

Shallote accompanied Clew and Jesse on their way back to the hotel. 'Young Brady Rawfield was in town this afternoon,' he informed them.

'We saw him,' Jesse replied. 'He was lookin' to kick the frost from somebody.'

'Yeah, his pa,' the ageing sheriff said. 'Turned out him an' Austen had one almighty row at the bank. We could hear the yellin' clear across the street.'

'I wonder if it was anything to do with the upcomin' auction?' Clew said.

Shallote left them then, to continue with his safeguarding tour of the town.

'What's troublin' you, Brother?' Clew asked at Jesse's continuing unease.

'This affair's gettin' me sort of drawn in. Don't you feel it?'

'Not really. They ain't friends or relatives. We ain't bein' consulted or retained, so why should I? But if *you're* goin' to get more involved, I guess I will, too.'

'I don't understand you sometimes, Clew.'

'Good. Look, Jesse, right now, we're bein'
paid to stay here an' screw down two killer
bank robbers. So you get turned in early an'
have someone call you at one. I'll be at the
jail until you show. You can stay until day-
break, OK?'

'Christ! Chapter an' Froote ain't got a
gang with 'em, Clew. There's no one goin' to
ride in an' break 'em out o' there.'

'I know that, Jesse. But I been thinkin'
about you an' your booger men ... them bad
things that happen at night. This time, I'd
rather do somethin' other than lie awake
wonderin'.'

13

At the hotel, Rowan Vine smiled good
humouredly as she mimed Jesse's breakfast
request of ham and eggs with tinned milk
and peaches.

'Are you satisfied or not?' he asked Clew,
after an uneventful night. 'That jail's closed
up tighter'n a mule's ass in a dust devil. It's
goin' to hold the likes o' Chapter an' Froote
for a day or two.'

'I'd like to think it's 'cause one of us was there,' Clew retorted. 'You can never be too certain, Jesse, never. Now, if you put that food away, we can buy ourselves a ticket up to Blue Peak.'

'Ah, come on, Clew. If anythin' happens up *there*, we'll be in the best place to find out, an' that's *here*. We'll go meet the train when we've had some coffee.'

When the south-bound train pulled in from Butte City, the first man to step down from the caboose was Rufus Maise. He was accompanied by the deputy marshal from Helena, and a reporter and staff photographer on the *Butte Examiner*. There were two other men of whom Jesse and Clew took watchful notice.

'Since we arrived, this shirt-tail outfit's become the hub o' the goddamn world,' Jesse remarked as, a short while later, they stood on the depot's jetty.

Maise arched his back, winced and groaned as he tried to ease out some stiffness.

'We hadn't expected to see you,' Clew said with genuine surprise, as he offered a hand to the bondsman.

'No, I don't expect you did,' Maise responded fractiously. 'With that degree of hardship, I'd be surprised if you ever got to see *anybody* arriving by train ... if you could call it that.'

'You came with the deputy?' Jesse asked.

'Yes. We've got the authority to remove the prisoners ... to renew their acquaintance with the Fort Hogback Penitentiary. An' there's the matter of the reward. Accordin' to your wire, the sheriff, John Shallote's entitled to it.'

'That he is,' Clew said. 'He wasn't there when we actually detained 'em, but most else was down to him.' Clew was being charitable, but the support of a sheriff was always useful in the Brannins' line of business. No need to create a grievance if you could afford not to.

'I'd like you boys to talk to the reporters,' Maise continued. 'I know it's not what you'd normally do – exactly the opposite in fact – but I did explain that we're taking our assault on bank raids seriously. This story can only help us.'

'Yeah, all right, but we ain't standin' in front of a camera,' Clew conceded. 'One question, Mr Maise. Who were the two other men who got off the train with you?'

'I don't know, they didn't introduce themselves. Maybe they're here for the auction.'

Clew looked a little unconvinced. 'Hmm.

But you musta been real hugger-mugger on the journey from Butte?'

'Yes, we were that all right. But I never spoke to anyone. I was too stiff and uncomfortable for my jaw to work at anything like talk. Ask the reporters, they'll likely know.'

'Don't know much,' one of the newspaper men said. 'They're pretty full of 'emselves. "Well known in Missoula", one of 'em told us.'

'Are they too high an' mighty for names?' Jesse asked mischievously.

'The one in the suit's Royston Brough. He's a banker, apparently. The other one's Noel Alliss, an attorney.'

'Yeah, ain't they all in Missoula,' Jesse sniggered

The Butte reporters, though, were understandably more interested in Clew and Jesse's exploits aboard the train. It was good for the circulation of their newspaper, exciting copy for their readers. When they wanted something more thrilling, they turned to John Shallote. But he told them they'd have to accompany him to his office.

'I got a deputy to take over from,' he said weightily. 'On the way we can call in on Milly Matches, make arrangements for you to file your story.'

'You turned in another excellent job, and the company's grateful,' Maise said, as he walked up the main street with Clew and Jesse.

'Thanks. You can pay us to that effect,' Clew suggested.

'I take it our responsibility for Chapter an' Froote's just ended?' Jesse enquired. 'An' by the way, where is that deputy marshal you brought with you?'

Maise grinned complacently. 'He's good, isn't he?' he replied. 'He's drifted into the background, but doing the job he's being paid for. You'll see him in the morning, when he turns in his authority to remove the prisoners. It does mean, of course, that we can't leave before the Saturday train. Will you two be leaving with us?'

'Normally, yeah,' Jesse said. 'But I'm kind o' lookin' forward to what happens here tomorrow. I'm thinkin' that, if this section of the line closes, there's goin' to be no link from here on up to Butte City.'

Maise's features expressed mild concern. 'Yes, I thought of that, and I've got mixed feelings about it. The company holds an account at the bank, so I'll probably be calling in on Austen Rawfield.'

Having a late meal, Brough and Alliss

94

were seated at Rowan Vine's other table.

'It might be wise to slip ol' John the word not to repeat anythin' we've picked up about this railway deal,' Clew said quietly to Jesse. 'I got a feelin' that before not too long, our fine-feathered friends there will also be meetin' up with Rawfield.'

'If they're up to somethin', they won't. Or if they think we're watchin' 'em.'

'What's for 'em to be suspicious about?' Clew wondered.

'I dunno. But they certainly ain't arrangin' a loan for Rawfield. An' they ain't here 'cause there's nothin' better for 'em to do.'

Outside of Hudson's Mercantile, the two Butte City newspaper men were sitting on the store bench, watching the town's shiftless movement. Clew and Jesse stopped to talk for a moment.

'Sorry about the pictures, boys, but havin' our true likenesses spread across the best part o' Montana don't help us,' Clew explained. 'But maybe we can offer you somethin' else ... somethin' to make up,' he offered.

'We're listenin', but let me guess. It concerns the sale o' some stove-up rail line an' a brake train,' Hedley Yves, the reporter, said dismissively.

'So it would seem,' Clew responded perceptively. 'But then why's two Missoula bigshots here to bid? You tell us that? With a financial interest in every railroad north o' the Mason-Dixon Line, what's a man like Royston Brough doin' down here?'

Jennings shrugged. 'Are you suggestin' there's a story ... we stay an' find out?'

Clew nodded. 'If I was a newspaper man, I just might. As you say, on the surface it's nothin' more'n a one-horse piece o' junk.'

'What's its interest to you two fellers?'

'We don't like seein' small folk squeezed. It's a problem we got ... can't seem to shake it,' Jesse replied.

'So you've got an idea o' what's *really* goin' on,' Yves alleged.

'I got an idea, sure,' Clew answered. 'It'll be what Alliss an' Brough are probably discussin' with Rawfield, while we sit here discussin' *them*.'

14

At Rufus Maise's request, Clew and Jesse met him and the deputy marshal at eleven o'clock the following morning. The circuit judge was presiding in the rear quarter of Hudson's Mercantile, where, with other local community business, he authorized the transfer of Duff Chapter and Gregor Froote. When Clew and Jesse stepped out of the store, they found that most of Whisper's populace were gathering for the auction.

'Don't see anythin' of our newspaper friends, though,' Jesse observed.

'They were wantin' word from their editors to stay. We can go back an' wait at Vine's.'

At 11.45 observers and all protagonists in the sale were milled outside of the store. Those who happened to pass by the hotel, looked stern and sober. 'Could the town itself be less interested?' Clew put to Jesse.

'Only if *nobody* turned up,' Jesse answered back.

But the townsfolk weren't the only interested parties. Cousin Pepper, Albert Cave and Dutch Barrow were three of the Snake Plain's ranch owners who had ridden in. A few cowboys had also turned up, but that was more out of concern for their livelihoods than anything else.

'Perhaps we should get on down there?' Jesse said.

'Yeah, an' I've just seen them newshounds. Let's go.'

'No word,' Hedley Yves said, shaking his head. 'But we'll stay on anyway. An' Miss Matches wants to be at the sale. We can't ask her to wait.'

Clew looked back along the street towards the depot, saw Milly with young Brady walking alongside her.

'Yeah, fair enough,' he said, 'let's get in there.'

Rufus Maise was waiting on the mercantile's veranda, and Austen Rawfield stood near with a dogged expression on his face. Alliss and Brough were to one side, but no obvious words were exchanged.

It was almost noon when John Shallote opened the door. He narrowed his eyes against the sun, checked his watch, and beckoned for everyone to enter the improvised court and sale-room.

'This ain't exactly one o' the Pacifics bein'

sold,' he called a moment or two later. 'So, by order, I'll get on with it. Actin' for the name of Hurd Growster, the line known to us all as the Growster-Matches Link is now up for sale. The highest bidder here today, gets *that,* together with rights o' way, rollin' stock, buildin's an' anythin' else associated with an' within its compass. Buyer takes on all payable bills, too.

'Right. Most o' you know the procedure, so, what am I bid?' he rapped out. 'What am I hearin'?'

'Four thousand dollars,' came immediately from Royston Brough.

Shallote gave the man a long, hard look. 'That's real close to stealin', mister,' he said. 'But I want another bid.'

'*Five* thousand,' Alliss called out.

Now that Shallote had the two bids required by law, the rail line was quickly very close to gone. 'I've been bid five thousand,' he reminded the men gathered around him. 'So, if you're through, I've got no—'

'Seven thousand dollars,' Jesse broke in, and to the amazement of not only Brough and Alliss, but all other potential bidders, Shallote immediately yelled, 'sold'.

'What the hell are you doin'?' Rawfield spluttered, and took a threatening step towards the sheriff. 'This auction's supposed to be run accordin' to law,' he ranted angrily. 'Open the biddin' an' give these other people a chance.'

Just as infuriated, Brough would have joined in the argument, but the cooler-headed Alliss restrained him.

'Those other men, as you call 'em, have had their chance, Austen,' Shallote flung back at Rawfield. 'I ain't called on to wait here all day for 'em to make up their minds. The line's sold to Jesse Brannin, an' that's final.'

'Mr Shallote,' the attorney, Noel Alliss, addressed the sheriff. 'The terms of the sale require a deposit of twenty-five per cent in cash, or by certified cheque, with the balance payable within thirty days. Can you please confirm that Mr Brannin is able to satis-factorily fulfil those terms?' he demanded with a testing glance at Jesse.

'There'll be a great big goddamn writ pinned to your ass if you're suggestin' that I ain't good for a few thousand dollars,' Jesse snapped back.

'I don't know *what* you're good for,' Alliss returned sharply. 'But if you knowingly entered into this auction without the funds to complete, then it's no sale.'

'Just a minute,' Rufus Maise spoke up, as

100

Rawfield appeared to side with Alliss. 'I'll be more than happy to take whatever payment Mr Brannin pleases, and in whatever form.'

Clew grabbed his brother's arm. 'Here's your chance to get out o' this,' he said under his breath. 'What the hell do you want with a goddamn railroad?'

'I don't know, Clew. I was tryin' to run up the figure to help Milly Matches out with some Growster compensation. But now I'm thinkin' of Jesse Brannin, railroad boss. Besides, that Missoula dude's a long way from home.'

When Milly approached Jesse, there was a tremble in her lower lip.

'Don't go upsettin' yourself, Miss Matches,' he said 'You're still in business. You just go on as you been doin'. If Rawfield or anyone else tries to give you a hard time, you let me know. Clew will take care of 'em.'

Clew shot his brother a surprised look.

'It's just that us railroad magnates don't go in for rough-housin',' Jesse kidded.

Milly smiled warmly and turned away without saying anything.

Very disgruntled, Rawfield had walked off with Alliss and Brough. But with their departure, John Shallote slapped a leathery old hand on Jesse's shoulder.

'Better a railroad than a pup, eh, Jesse?' he cackled.

'That's a favourable way o' lookin' at it,' Jesse conceded. 'I mean, you could've gone on with the biddin'.'

'I could, yeah. But them fellers'll make you an offer before the day's through, or I'm a Dutchman.' Then he jerked his head in Maise's direction. 'You get the cash, Mr Maise, an' we'll close on the sale.'

Maise nodded. 'We'll meet at the bank, sometime,' he said. 'You let me have your cheque, Jesse, and I'll endorse it or get the cash. How much are you wanting to pay now?'

'All of it,' Jesse responded. 'I ain't been savin' for five years to end up not ownin' a goddamn railroad.'

Clew knew it was the truth about the money. Over the same period of time, he, too, had saved a similar amount. But ten minutes later, when he was alone with Jesse, he voiced an anxious thought.

'This just about beats every one of the idiotic things you done in your life, Jesse,' he said. 'Are you goin' to ask Milly Matches to run your railroad?'

'I don't rightly know what I'm goin' to do. But I can't think of anyone who'd do a better job. No one knows better than *her*, how it shakes up.'

'It's your money, Jesse, but I reckon your feelin's are runnin' ahead o' good sense.'

'Look, Clew, if you want to get back to Bozeman, to chase them big fat retainers, it's OK with me.'

'Hah, I'm not goin' anywhere for the moment, Jesse. With you now ownin' a railroad, *this* is where them fat retainers are more likely to be. But, right this minute, I'm shinin' up my gun, 'cause I got a feelin' we might be needin' it.'

They'd taken a seat outside of the mercantile, were talking of visiting the bank, when Jesse noticed Royston Brough returning. 'Maybe sooner than you think, Brother,' was his considered answer to Clew.

'I'd like a word, Mr Brannin,' Brough said stepping up to the veranda.

Jesse immediately thought of what John Shallote had said about being a Dutchman. 'What kept you?' he returned with a weary smile.

'I'll get straight to the point,' Brough said, with the terseness of someone used to having his way, of someone important in Missoula. 'Are you interested in a quick profit on today's transaction?'

Jesse took a deep, noisy intake of air. 'Are *you*, Mr Brough?' he asked back. 'I mean, ain't *that* why you're here?'

'I'll give you ten thousand for the line an' it's stock,' Brough railed.

Though he was more than tempted to say yes, Jesse shook his head whilst Clew cursed under his breath. 'I ain't interested,' he bluffed. 'I got some other plans.'

'I'll make it fifteen. An' to grease the wheels, so to speak, I'll consider whatever plans you had in mind, like the retainin' of a telegraph an' goods depot.'

Jesse shook his head slowly. 'I ain't interested,' he repeated with quiet caution.

'You're out for a high price,' Brough said, 'so I won't haggle any more. I'll give you twenty-five thousand cash.'

Clew saw the wound up danger from his brother and suddenly moved forward. 'Look, mister, if the line's worth twenty-five thousand to you, it's worth twenty-five thousand to us,' he rasped. 'Be smart an' accept you just gone an' lost a deal.'

Brough clenched his fists. Unaccustomed to losing, he was taken aback, momentarily unsettled.

'Don't sleep soundly thinkin' you're getting the better of me,' he warned.

Clew smiled, turned away from the businessman who was already pacing irately back along the street. 'I think we already have,' he said dismissively. 'An' as I was sayin'. I got me a gun needs cleanin'.'

15

'You called me some kind of idiot for buyin' up that pile o' rusted junk. Well, what do you reckon now?' Jesse asked of his brother.

'Dependin' on what you got in mind, I could still be right, if you're aimin' to resurrect it.'

'Yeah? So what was all the "we" business with Brough? If it's the "we" I think you mean, you can write me a cheque for three an' a half thousand dollars, right now.'

'Yep, I'm with you, Brother, equal partners. If I learn to shoot left-handed, I'll even fight to keep what we bought,' Clew offered. 'Meantime, let's go see if we can find them reporters. Best not mention about Brough's offer though: that's *our* business.'

'Be interestin' to know what Brough's next move is,' Jesse wondered. 'He's goin' to make one, that's for sure. He ain't one to make idle threats.'

'He'll most likely come back with another offer when he's cooled down. What if he ups it to fifty grand?'

'That's OK with me,' Jesse said. 'Maybe we could let Milly have a slice o' the cake.'

At the depot, they found Hedley Yves and the photographer seated atop a packing box enjoying the warm spring sunshine. In the nearby office, the telegraph receiver was clicking busily.

'Sounds like someone's got somethin' to say,' Jesse said.

Milly Matches leaned from her office window. 'Message for you, Mr Yves,' she called out.

Yves glanced at it quickly, looked puzzled as he started to speak. 'Listen to this, see if it makes sense,' he said. 'Brough, Alliss and Co building Jackson Ford spur line. No plans disclosed yet. Possible link through. Get confirmation. Send anything you can get.'

The reporter re-read the message carefully. 'Buildin' the Jackson spur. Possible link through? Through to what? What the hell does that lot mean?'

'It means, linkin' with our defunct Growster-Matches line,' Clew said thoughtfully.

'An that means, if they finish diggin' the tunnel north o' Blue Peak, there'll be a connection straight to Livingstone. It's a venture they've given up on two or three times already 'cause o' the cost. But that wouldn't be an issue with Royston Brough's money behind it.'

'Where's the tunnel, Clew?' Jesse asked.

'Beaverheads, north o' Blue Peak.'

'I've got a map,' Milly said.

Milly came from the office with a map of Montana's tract of the Northern Pacific Railroad. It stretched from Missoula in the west to Miles City in the east.

'There's big snows up there, an' gradients,' Jesse suggested.

'Yeah, they'd need a few miles o' snow sheds either side o' Blue Peak, if they want to keep the line open,' Milly said.

'But what's the main plan?' Jesse asked.

'It's plain enough, Jesse,' Milly said. 'My pa often talked about it. It's more a less a giant box line that gives Butte City an' Blue Peak equal access to the Northern Pacific. An' *that* brings *us* in.'

Jesses and Clew's eyes narrowed with interest and deliberation.

'From Livingstone, you'll be able to drop right down to Blue Peak,' Milly continued.

'No need to go on to Garrison an' Butte City. An' that's worth the savin' of nearly two days.'

'An' how do we figure?' Clew knew, but wanted the confirmation.

'If we're in, we're the icin' on the cake. If we're out, we're dead.'

'So won't the Northern Pacific be after it ... us?' Jesse asked.

'Yeah, 'course they will be. Up till now, the Growster-Matches Link's the only workable route for a line through Snake Plain.'

'Who does Alliss represent?' Clew asked the reporter. 'Do you know?'

'Yeah, that's no secret – the Northern Pacific Railroad.'

'Ha. Now that we own their golden goose, fifty grand's lookin' like small peas,' Jesse grinned.

'Has Brough already made you an offer?' Yves asked.

'That's a question best put to him,' Jesse said quickly.

'I will then,' Yves decided, and left immediately to try and find out.

Clew and Jesse took over the packing box seat with Milly. Jesse told her that Clew now held an equal interest in the line, and that she was to consider herself as a regular partner.

'I do thank you for that. But why?' she asked modestly.

'Er, we like you, ma'am,' Clew answered. 'Well, I do. Jesse just sees you more as a fair investment,' he joshed.

The three of them sat silent and pleased for a minute, watched as the various ranchers pulled out of town, back to their ranches on the Snake Plain.

'I reckon we best keep the lid on any thoughts o' cuttin' loose,' Clew offered calmly.

'Why? Who's to object to a bit o' celebratin'?' Jesse asked.

'All the big brass nuts who've just had their noses put out o' joint, that's who. If you imagine all the dynamite that's needed to blast through the Blue Peak tunnel, right now we're probably sittin' on top of it,' Clew suggested plainly. 'Soon we're goin' to be offered more money than Royston Brough could raise in ten lifetimes. An' when we say "no sale", their attorney's goin' to light the fuse. We're goin' to have to do somethin' other than hide all the goddamn matches.'

16

Clew and Jesse spent nearly an hour with Milly discussing the immediate requirements of the line.

'We got to pay up them back taxes that Shallote mentioned,' Jesse said. 'Somethin' that Growster must have let slip.'

'The tracks ain't in great shape, but as long's we don't put too much stress on it, it'll last a bit,' Milly said wryly. 'I've been talkin' with Brady. He says he's come to the end of his tether with his pa, an' he's movin' into town. He said the ranchers that came to the auction are the ones in debt to the bank. Dutch Barrow's got a mortgage, an' he was wonderin' how to pay it off. If Whisper loses the railroad, the value of his place will be cut in two. Albie Cave an' Cousin Pepper feel about the same.'

'But that ain't all bad,' Clew suggested. 'It'll give 'em a reason to help us when needs be. Tell young Brady to get 'em lined up. Next week, we'll get together with Enoch Hudson, an' any other merchants left in town. We'll see if they'll give us *some* backin'.'

'Yeah, OK. You know someone's goin' to be watchin', so where do you want to have the meetin'?' Milly wanted to know.

'In Hudson's Mercantile. Every other get-together seems to happen there. Wouldn't want anyone to feel left out. An' if Brough or Alliss have anythin' to say, they can come find us.'

'Where we goin' to be then?' Jesse asked

'If we knew that, they wouldn't have to find us, would they?' Clew reasoned.

They were in John Shallote's office at the jail that evening, together with Rufus Maise and the deputy marshal from Helena, when Noel Alliss called by.

'I'd like to go back to the hotel an' talk things over with you,' he said to the Brannins.

'We haven't anythin' to say, that can't be said here,' Jesse claimed. 'Ain't you talkin' to Brough? He could've told you how we felt about the offer.'

'I'm afraid you gentlemen are barkin' up the wrong tree,' the attorney countered. 'If you think we're goin' to keep on makin' increased offers, until we meet your price, then think again. We've got two men up at Blue Peak who've told us that we don't have to blast through a tunnel, or even link up with your wretched rail line. No, we can take a road bed *around* the Peak. It's certainly goin' to cost extra, but not as much as you're hangin' out for. So that leaves you an' Whisper to wither an' die. A question of greed overreachin' itself, I think.'

Clew realized immediately that the two men whom they'd been told were prospecting for Austen Rawfield, were, in fact, employees of the Northern Pacific Railroad.

'Mr Brough and I are leavin' for Missoula in the mornin',' Alliss continued. 'So here's one final offer for old-time's sake: fifty thousand.'

'You ain't much of a judge o' human nature, are you?' Jesse put to Alliss. 'We really ain't interested in the money. It's the goddamn rail line we want.'

'Yeah, an' besides that, any *real* offer would have to include certain guarantees which are beyond even your combined purse,' Clew added.

'Like what?' Alliss queried.

'Like you rebuildin' the town. Makin' Whisper somethin' more'n fly dirt on a map.'

Alliss dismissed that with a wave of his hand. 'As I said, you're goin' to wither an' die. But now you got nowhere to go.' With that, the attorney turned on his heel, left in the same piqued manner as Royston Brough had earlier in the day.

With slightly bewildered looks on their faces, the brothers looked at each other. 'Fifty thousand,' they murmured, almost in unison. 'Jeez, what we gone an' done, Clew?' Jesse said, after a confused moment. 'Rawfleld could have had the line for ten thousand, if he'd offered it straight to Growster. What do you reckon their next move'll be?'

'I think there'll be another offer. But they'll try an' soften us up before they make it. We got to think, act careful. Two men lookin' for precious metals, my ass.'

In the morning, Chapter and Froote were shackled by the deputy marshal before being led to the early train. Brough and Alliss were already seated in wicker chairs in the caboose. Clew was of a mind to go and see them off, say that the best men had won. But he decided that their direct departure was enough.

With Jesse, Rufus Maise and John Shallote, he walked to the depot where they shook hands with the reporters.

'Keep an eye out for the Missoula press,' Hedley Yves suggested. 'If you ever happen to hit town, come see us.'

Early afternoon saw Clew and Jesse on their way up Blue Peak. Doc Kelso had found Clew's arm nearly healed.

'Completely, if I take it out o' this goddamn sling,' was Clew's frank opinion.

Using the hand cart from the pass junction, Jesse took much of the strain, and had managed to thrust them up to the peak in less than two hours. Clew wanted to size up the men who were employed there, take a look at whoever else might have arrived.

Will McGirty, the foreman ganger, told them that they all knew the happenings of the previous day in Whisper. 'We had someone come up an' tell us,' he said. 'We all like to keep informed o' the local horse tradin'.'

'Yeah, well, this is *iron-horse* tradin',' Jesse said, taking a look around. 'What work are you boys doin' up here?'

'Track maintenance ... shorin' up the creek,' he answered, a bit guardedly.

'You'll be needin' a lot bigger gang, if there's ever major work to be done,' Clew suggested.

'If ever, yeah,' the man agreed with a cautious smile. 'What do *you* know?'

'What everyone else does – that there's a deal about to be cut with the Northern an' Pacific. I hear they've already got a couple of agents up here. There's likely to be some hostility. How are you all set for that?'

'Ha. I don't know whether you seen long saws an' axes put to improper use, mister. But let me tell you it ain't a pretty sight. 'Specially when they're in the hands of a few crazy Irishmen.'

Both Jesse and Clew were impressed, but their features remained impassive. 'If you need more hands, hire 'em. No waitin' for wages. There'll be fightin' pay up front,' Clew promised.

The tie-man gave Clew then Jesse a penetrating look. 'You'll be the Brannins, then,' he said.

'Yeah, I'm Jesse, this is Clew,' Jesse told him. 'The new owners o' the stretch o' rail line that brought us up here. The ones you might be swingin' them axes for.'

The man nodded thoughtfully. 'Them two fellers you mentioned are long gone. They were chummed up with some timber markers though, an' *they* ain't.'

'Timber markers? Clew said surprisedly. 'Sounds as if someone's jumpin' the gun. Point out where them two scouts were quartered. We'd like to see if there's anythin' left behind.'

17

In the small pine cabin that had been occupied until recently by the two so-called prospectors, Clew and Jesse found the evidence they were looking for. 'I reckon they should've burned this stuff before hightailin' it,' Clew said. 'Alliss sure wouldn'ta wanted us layin' eyes on this. There's nothin' that looks anythin' like a reference to the minin' o' precious metals, or any other goddamn ores. It's routes for excavatin' an' blastin'. These are plans about track layin' around the peak. An' *that's* what the timber markers are doin'.'

Clew and Jesse were so held by the bits and pieces of charts and drawings, that they didn't see the big man approaching. The man sidled into the doorway of the cabin, his eyes blazing menacingly when he saw what was being looked over.

'What the hell you doin' with them papers?' His rough, aggressive voice resonated around the cabin walls.

'I'm Jesse Brannin,' Jesse said calmly. 'So, by my reckonin', whatever I'm doin' with these papers, is my business. In fact, most anythin' that goes on up here's my business one way or another.'

'Yeah, I figured who you might be when I saw you climb off that hand car. But it don't change anythin'. So, put them papers down an' get out.'

'Hold up one moment. Who the hell are you sided with?' Clew asked.

'We're paid by the Northern Pacific.'

'Well, I'm real sorry to hear that, mister. But meantime, we got ourselves a very important date with the telegraph back in Whisper. So you're just goin' to have to stand aside,' Jesse said, with little room for misunderstanding.

'I don't stand aside for anyone,' the big man threatened.

'Yeah, I thought you'd say that. But if you'll just let me through, I'll present you with a better set o' credentials,' Jesse said, brushing past the bemused man.

Jesse walked thirty feet from the cabin before turning around. The big man had advanced a couple of stubborn paces, and it was Clew who now stood in the doorway.

'If ever we have to take you in for trespass, I'll want to know your name,' Jesse said.

'Cargo. An' what's the goddamn credentials you're talkin' about?'

'These. Never go anywhere without 'em,' Jesse said, and raised a clenched fist. Then he quickly unbuckled his gunbelt and tossed it to Clew. As he closed in on Cargo he cursed under his breath for not giving more consideration to returning to Bozeman.

When Jesse was at arm's length, Cargo jutted his heavily bearded chin and sneered, 'You just started a big, big mistake.'

Hardly a muscle moved in Jesse's face. He lashed out very quickly with his right fist, and Cargo's head went back like a cow-pen hinge. His lips were splitting tight against his jaw of rot-coloured teeth, and when his shoulders, backside and heels hit the ground flat out, Jesse was on him.

Cargo was badly shaken, but his tough instinct for survival was still working. He cursed, half turned, flung an arm around Jesse's neck, and clung tight. Jesse's knuckles drove into the back of the man's grease-caked head, but the man swung himself over. Face down, he rose to get onto all-fours, and with brute strength, reached for another neck grip.

Jesse dodged him and threw all his weight forward. Cargo collapsed into the attack and together they rolled over and over through loose shale. They were struggling for an advantage, clawing for each other as ferocious and ruthless as a distraught grizzly.

They managed to climb to their feet, stood toe to toe, shocking each other with their enraged punches. Blood was pouring from their mouths and noses as Cargo snapped them into a clinch. They staggered from side to side, backwards and forwards before going down heavily, with Jesse underneath. The man thrust his left forearm under Jesse's chin and with the fingers of his right hand gouged at his eyes. Jesse lifted a leg as high as he could with his heel against Cargo. He kicked inward and thrust his boot back down sharply. With a bellow of pain Cargo flung himself away, staggered to regain his balance. One leg of his trousers had been ripped open, and blood streamed from where Jesse's prick spur had torn its way through.

They quartered the ground as they fought, sometimes throwing punches, sometimes manoeuvring for a handhold. Their lungs began to labour and rasp, and they staggered in unbalanced circles. Eventually, the muscles in their arms lost control, and their legs dragged heavily.

Cargo was the bigger and stronger man, but he lacked the guile and thoughtful purpose of Jesse. Watching cautiously, Jesse knew that if the fight went on much longer, they'd both go down. But it would be the one who went down first, who'd stay there longest.

Cargo was slumping now, could hardly lift his fists. He fought only in futile, defensive spurts, and as if to prove it, he lowered his head and went forward in one last despairing attack. A lucky aimless blow flung Jesse across the trunk of a stunted pine and, thrashing even more wildly, the man plunged forward to try and finish the fight.

But Jesse was still thinking and he ducked, twisting quickly to one side. Cargo missed with his punch and rolled hard around the gnarled bark. Jesse grunted, eased himself back and settled for grabbing as much of the man's hair and ears as he could. He drew Cargo's head back and smashed his face, just once, solidly against the ridges of crusty bark.

The body of the man gave out and he sank to the ground, his head falling to the shallow creek that curled close around the roots of the tree. Breathless, Jesse lost his balance, and he fell exhausted on top of Cargo. For a short time, both men lay without stirring, then nearly gagging at the raw, beastly stench that wept from the man's body, Jesse pushed himself away. But he stopped when he noticed the man's shattered face was under the water, crushing against the bed pebbles. He gripped the damp leather jacket around the man's shoulders, and exerting his remaining strength, dragged Cargo's upper body clear of the water.

Taking support from the stunted pine, Jesse looked down at the swollen, bruised face of the man he'd been fighting with. But he was too weary for any sentiment and, regaining his footing, he wiped his face with his wet hands and painfully climbed back up the low, shelving bank.

'There was a time when our ma would have given you a fat ear for comin' home after a scrap like that,' Clew said, handing back Jesse's gunbelt. 'An' you've got your feet wet.'

'Well, the man was spoilin' for a fight, an' I guess I was too.'

'But what were you fightin' *about?*' Clew asked. 'I kind've forgot in the excitement.'

'He wouldn't get out o' the way.'

Clew nodded. 'Perhaps he'll see there ain't much future in that, an' change sides.'

'We takin' him back to the car?' Jesse asked. 'We can use him as cover.'

'Yeah, why not. We'll roll him off when we've picked up speed. You hear *that*, Cargo?

You're comin' for a short ride.'

'There'll be some other time.' Cargo spat and dribbled the words into his beard.

'I hope so, feller,' Clew said. 'I'd hate for you to get killed in the fall.'

18

'I expected somethin' o' the sort,' Brady Rawfield said, when Clew recalled the presence of Max Cargo and his men up at Blue Peak. 'I didn't expect it quite so soon though. But we can run 'em out. Say the word, an' I can round up some men.'

'We'll have to be sure of our ground before we try that,' Clew replied. 'If the land *is* sold, they'll have a legal right to be there. With a battery o' high price lawyers to throw at us, the Northern Pacific'll just be waitin' for us to step outside o' the law.'

'*Their* law, more like,' Milly Matches said, frustrated and angered by the news.

'I agree, Milly, an' I'd like nothin' more'n to get up there an' run 'em out. But we'll watch 'em, an' if they lay a hand on our trains or property, we'll go after 'em.'

'What else are they there for, if not that?' Milly asked.

'To look after the surveyors that Brough put up there. He was reckonin' on ownership of our rail line, don't forget.'

Together, they pieced together the papers they'd found up at the cabin. 'See, they don't intend to get near enough to Whisper for us to see 'em wave,' Clew pointed out.

'Yeah,' Jesse acknowledged. 'An' that's somethin' for you to keep in mind when you get out on the Plain,' he told Brady.

'It's a strong argument. You couldn't have a stronger one for gettin' your Snake Plain friends together for a meetin',' Clew said. 'I'll take a look to see if there's a lodged deed. There should be somethin' there. It won't be before Monday, though. It would look like breakin' an' enterin', even with Hudson's collusion.'

'Why wait till then? Why don't we go see him now?' Jesse asked. 'If he's agreeable to turnin' his back, we can take a look through the records, an' hit the Plain with Brady tomorrow. We can hold the meetin' Monday night.'

'I appreciate what you're askin', friends, but the mercantile's my business, an' I'd like to hang on to it for as long as possible, but if I let you run amok among county records, I won't for much longer. Monday'll be soon enough,' Hudson responded to Jesse's idea. 'Meantime though, I'll see who else I can get to go with us.

'You won't have any trouble linin' up Dutch an' Albie Cave an' the rest of 'em,' he went on. 'Tell 'em to show up at the store Monday evenin' at eight. When they hear the news of what's happenin' up at Blue Peak, I wouldn't want to be in Austen Rawfield's boots.'

'He's too far down the chain to be our biggest worry,' Clew said. 'He's no more'n that Missoula gang's errand boy.'

Sunday was a clear and warm day. Up in the Beaverheads, the snow was beginning its withdrawal from the timbered slopes.

Clew and Jesse went to collect their horses from where they'd been stabled at the town barn. They met Brady Rawfield, and from there, the three men rode out to Dutch Barrow's ranch.

Barrow wasn't a man who needed much persuasion. 'An ox train couldn't keep me away,' he exclaimed with a keen laugh.

The riders met with an equally enthusiastic reaction from Albie Cave and Cousin

Pepper. 'We'll have a good crowd gathered tomorrow night,' Jesse said. 'Let's hope you can find them deeds.'

'Yeah,' Clew sounded a shade apprehensive. 'Remember, deeds don't have to be recorded promptly. With a sweetener, stuffs easy buried.'

'If you don't find anythin', we'll find out why, by doin' the same,' Brady said.

Monday morning brought the money order the Brannins had requested from the Bozeman Municipal Bank. They also picked up their personal traps that had come by stagecoach and rail from Pony Flats.

'While you're out back o' the mercantile, I'll go an' open up a bank account,' Jesse grinned. 'As a new customer, I wonder if Rawfield'll offer me coffee an' cake?'

A half-hour later, outside of Hudson's Mercantile, Jesse eagerly asked what Clew had found.

'Austen Rawfield's got the right to build from Blue Peak, north to Jackson Ford. He filed two months ago,' Clew said impassively.

Jesse hadn't considered the immediate consequences. 'What do we do now?' he asked.

'Go see John Shallote, an' get his take on it. It's still his administration.'

The old sheriff was half asleep in his office. Clew told him about Max Cargo moving into Blue Peak. 'They're callin' 'emselves timber markers,' he said.

'This is the goddamn first I heard of it,' Shallote responded drowsily. 'I guess I'll have to find out what right they've got to be up there, if any.'

'They might have one, John. I've just come from lookin' at the recorded deed. Austen Rawfield's the owner of the Blue Peak property, an' Max Cargo an' his men have got pay an' permission to be there.'

'Hmm. I hear you got a gather at the mercantile,' Shallote said.

'An' you're welcome, John,' Clew replied. 'We didn't ask you 'cause we thought you might be compromised by your bein' sheriff.'

Shallote thought the predicament over for a moment. 'Yeah, perhaps I better steer clear,' he said. 'But you got my support. I ain't hidin' behind no badge. Whisper's supported me for long enough.'

'You best get your position sorted, Sheriff,' Jesse advised. 'We're lockin' horns with just about the most powerful corporation in Montana. Kind of makes you go weak at the knees, don't it?'

Milly nodded a solemn, silent agreement.

'How long will your meetin' at Hudson's last?' she asked Clew.

'Not long. I'll ask Brady to call in an' see you afterwards. Not that he wouldn't anyway, eh?'

Milly gave a jaded smile. 'I wouldn't take that for granted, Clew,' she said. 'It's not goin' to be easy for him, with his father an' all. They ain't goin' to be singin' *his* praises.'

'Of *that* you can be sure, Milly,' Jesse agreed emphatically. 'But if Brady's there, perhaps folk'll run around any personal stuff.'

Later, after supper, Clew and Jesse sat talking. 'I can't believe we're in this,' Jesse muttered, a bemused look in his eyes. 'Seems like we're actin' out the story for some goddamn dime novel.'

'Well, whatever it turns out to be, it was *you*, Brother, who got us into it.'

'Yeah, an' you said you'd stick with me 'cause I owned a railroad, as I recall.'

'It's you with the doubts, Jesse,' Clew said with a wry smile. 'Let's just hope the story turns out to be a twist on David an' Goliath. Now get your feet back on the ground, an' we'll drift across to the mercantile.'

19

Outside of Hudson's store, a small handful of men were waiting. But by eight o' clock, more than twenty were present, Brady Rawfield among them. Enoch Hudson moved to the rear of his store, got their attention and called the meeting to order.

'I'll make this part real short an' let Clew Brannin do the talkin',' he said and moved aside.

Clew gave a brief account and without any elaboration of what his and Jesse's Blue Peak survey had revealed.

'Goddamn crook,' Dutch Barrow exploded. 'He would've paid bottom dollar for that land ... land you can't grow nothin' on.'

'I think you're missin' the point, Mr Barrow,' Clew said. 'Unless it's for ties and rails, the land ain't for growin'. Rawfield gettin' it for peanuts ain't any problem either. It's what happens after the line's put down, that matters.'

'You mean, openin' up Blue Peak, an' puttin' all the resources into creatin' some newfangled settlement?' Hudson said.

'Yeah, somethin' like that,' Clew admitted. 'Whisper's days'll be over. No trade, an' property won't be worth a plugged nickel. Alliss's idea o' witherin' an' dyin's about right.'

'I was the first stockman to run cattle onto the Plain,' Albert Cave put in. 'Whenever I got me some spare money, I bought more land ... me an' ol' Pepper here. So much for our smart move, eh? We get to lose just about everythin'.'

'We can't ever prove it, 'cause he's long gone already, but who's to say that Hurd Growster weren't ever part of all this?' Cousin Pepper suggested.

'Well, if he *was*, I hope he's usin' my goddamn money to grubstake a long ways from here,' Jesse said.

'We'll all be pullin' up to Blue Peak for most everythin' we need,' Barrow exclaimed. 'If Rawfield has got the beatin' of us, I'm tellin' you it won't be for long. I ain't losin' my life's work for no goddamn land chiseller. No sir.'

Amid the tetchy remonstration that followed, the bell pinged when the front door of the mercantile opened. The clamour dropped, and heads turned to see Austen

Rawfield enter the store.

'You better listen to what I got to say,' Rawfield shouted without any preamble. 'You've already let a couple o' strangers buy their way into your town. I don't much care what you think o' me, but it would be mighty short-ranged if you didn't let the other side o' the coin have its say.'

The small gathering sniffed and shuffled unresponsively. Clew thought the business-man was looking around for his son, but Brady was hiding tactfully behind a stack of packing crates.

'For years I've hoped to give Snake Plain a proper railroad,' Rawfield went on. 'You've watched the railway company goin' from bad to worse. It's down to one worn-out mornin' train that takes more'n a full day to get anywhere. An' as for passenger seatin', there's some lines got better accommodation for livestock.'

'Yeah, we know that, but what about our town? What about Whisper?' Enoch Hudson wanted to know.

'Blue Peak's goin' to be the makin' of the Plain, an' the cattle business it supports. Sure there's goin' to be some changes. Where in the world ain't there? It's a fine, sheltered location with a clean run o' water.

It'll be fast down to your stockyards, an' fast up to Butte City, Garrison or Livingstone. How many o' you have actually *seen* the camp?'

'Up till now, there ain't been no reason to,' Dutch Barrow said.

'Yeah,' Jesse agreed. 'An' those of us that have been up there met with a curious kind o' reception committee,' he said, touching the bruises along his jaw line.

'What's the goin' rate for a store lot, in a town that you own?' Hudson asked.

Rawfield's look became less accommodating. 'It's the rail company that's plannin' the town. They'll be promotin' it ... givin' incentives to encourage its growth,' he said.

'I think we heard all we want to know about Blue Peak, Mr Rawfield. We'll come to our own conclusions. We're grateful to you for droppin' by.' Enoch Hudson's words effectively concluded the meeting.

'I've got one more thing to say,' Clew said, when Rawfield had gone. 'Jesse an' me buyin' our way into your town's one way o' lookin' at what happened, but if Austen Rawfield's right, we ain't gettin' much return from an' up an' comin' ghost town. Just remember *who else* was at the auction, an' got powerful snorty when *they* didn't get

131

to buy in. Mr Rawfield's in the dark, fellers, an' right now he's passin' the lamp around.'

'I don't see anyone much supportin' our cause,' Albert Cave said.

'How do we help ourselves?' Barrow asked Clew.

'By just doin' it. An' come runnin' when you're needed.'

A few men stood around talking, looking for safety and confidence in their number. It was nearly ten o' clock when Clew and Jesse were alone with Brady.

'We promised Milly we'd send you around to tell her what happened,' Clew said. 'Might not be seemly if you leave it much later.'

'Is there anythin' in particular you want me to tell her?'

'Just tell her that these people are standin' with us. Let her know we got the backin' o' thirty, if we need 'em.'

'Thirty?' Jesse queried incredulously.

'Just tell her, Brady,' Clew said.

20

Will McGirty sent a man down to Whisper to let the Brannins know that he'd hired reinforcements for his tie cutting and patch-up gang. Clew and Jesse were still in the depot when John Shallote rode up.

'I just seen Brady,' he started excitedly. 'Looked to me like he was on his way up to the Peak. He was kickin' somethin' out of that roan o' his, but I saw he had his rifle. I ain't his keeper, Jesse, but what's wrong?'

'Plenty. Cargo an' his men are a no good bunch o' varmints, an' you know it. If they spot him, they'll likely shoot him from the saddle.'

'Don't underestimate the boy, John. I'll wager his ol' man taught him how to take care of himself.'

The sheriff didn't look too certain. 'I'm sayin' that anythin' you wanted to know about the doin's up there, you could've asked *me*. That's where I'm goin'.'

'That's good, John, but you won't see anythin' o' young Brady. He'll be keepin' his

133

head down.'

'Yeah, that's what I'm afraid of. Keepin' his head down alongside the breech of a Winchester .44.'

'Rawfield don't own the whole goddamn mountain,' Jesse chipped in. 'The Brady boy could be up there huntin' for a big cat, for what anyone else knows.'

Shallote cast a penetrating eye on the Brannins. 'Listen to me good,' he warned. 'If you two are up to somethin' scrubby, I want in on it, you hear?'

Clew smiled good-naturedly. 'Yeah, we hear you, John,' he said. 'If it's shootin' you're talkin' about, you'll be the first to know, even if you ain't the first to be invited.'

'I'm sorry about this, Milly,' Shallote apologized to Milly who was looking quietly and fittingly worried. 'I just don't want the boy gettin' himself into trouble.'

'I'm sure *none* of us do,' Milly said.

'Are you boys headed up there?' Shallote asked them.

Clew nodded. 'Sometime tomorrow.'

'Then look me up this evenin'. I'll let you know how I make out with Max Cargo.'

'Just don't stand too close,' Jesse mocked.

'What was the apology to Milly all about?' he asked, after the sheriff had ridden off.

'I'm not sure. I could guess, though.'

'Go on.'

'He's probably thinkin' that *we* sent Brady up there to do some damage. That by stayin' here in town, we get ourselves the alibi.'

'Huh, shame that ain't the truth of it,' Jesse said. 'We weren't goin' up there to-morrow, were we?'

'No. But *now* we'll have to.'

Milly was thinking about what Clew and Jesse were saying. 'I heard someone say they've got no fire breaks up there. If a fire was to strike, they'd all lose their cabins,' she said after several moments.

'Yeah, it don't bear thinkin' about, Milly,' Clew said. There was a glint in his eye, because he thought maybe Milly was wait-ing for him to readily agree. 'But it wouldn't achieve much, other than givin' Max Cargo an' his crew a cold night.'

Milly smiled and went back to the tele-graph office a little more assured.

Clew and Jesse saw John Shallote as first dark was falling across the town. The old sheriff told them that he'd seen nothing of Brady on his ride up to Blue Peak.

'We told you as much,' Jesse said, 'But what about Max Cargo? Did you see him?'

'Yeah. He said they're runnin' out o' food.'

'Huh, I'd be surprised if he can get down anythin' more'n slumgullion.'

'You hear anythin' else?' Clew asked.

'It was mentioned that if anythin' goes wrong – if there's any trouble – as owners o' the line, *you're* responsible. The Northern Pacific will throw everythin' at you, an' they'll win.'

'If they need to freight stuff from the Peak, what's the purpose in either of us makin' trouble?' Jesse pondered.

'They've got to get most o' the blastin' an' track laid before winter sets in. It's more about delay than trouble,' the sheriff informed them.

'An' meantime we got to carry on acceptin' freight, an' lettin' 'em stop us on a flag?' Jesse questioned.

'Yeah. But if we can't beat 'em, we'll goddamn join 'em ... sort of,' Clew said.

Jesse grinned cruelly. 'Yeah, *then* beat the stuffin' out of 'em,' he promised. 'We'll get pitched into 'em long before they start round the Peak.'

That afternoon, Brady Rawfield spotted Clew and Jesse as they started their climb from the flatlands. Realizing they were looking for him, he rode a trail down a pine-timbered shoulder of the Peak to intercept them.

'I had a spyglass on 'em most o' yesterday an' today,' Brady said. 'I counted six. Half of 'em are livin' in one cabin. The rest are bunkin' in one alongside.'

'So, what do they do?' Clew asked about Max Cargo and his henchmen.

'Nothin' much. They barely stir … must be like hogs in muck. I saw one of 'em sittin' by the creek tryin' to catch a trout. I don't know what they got in them cabins, but there can't be too much grub. That was more or less when John Shallote showed up. What was he doin'?'

'He thinks you came up here to fire the place. An' it was us that sent you,' Jesse responded with a broad smile of devilment.

'Did they try to flag the down train early this mornin'?' Clew asked.

'I think they did, yeah,' Brady said. 'They must've wanted to come into town. Ha, but ol' Liam gave 'em the bum's rush.'

'Good,' Clew said. 'Accordin' to the sheriff, they'll be wantin' to stock up on food supplies. What else did you see, Brady?'

'I saw the big feller, Max Cargo. Him an' a couple of others went to have a look at what the tie-cutters were doin'. They kept 'emselves well hidden though. I reckon there'll be folk willin' to pay good money for a ticket when that lot tangles. Oh, an' some other men got off the train, too. I couldn't see where they went, or who they spoke to. But they didn't look like any sort o' workforce.'

'McGirty an' his men can look after 'emselves,' Jesse said confidently.

'One of us better go tell the engine crew they'll be gettin' visitors some night,' Clew decided. 'An' they'll be up for fightin' wages. You mind stickin' it out here a while longer, Brady? We brought some o' Rowan's best fixin's for you.'

'Yeah, OK. I probably got another day in me. How's Milly?'

'I wondered when you'd ask,' Clew flipped back. 'She's just fine. She's warmin' to the idea o' supplyin' ties to the Northern Pacific.'

'What? Ain't that a bit like diggin' your own grave?'

'Not necessarily, Brady. Appearances can be deceivin'.'

It was only first dark, when Max Cargo and his men removed the wedges from the wheels of two flatcars. It took them a further two minutes to release the brakes. Man-handling did the rest, and the cars began to move off. That was when the noise from the rolling stock alerted the camp at Blue Peak, and, too late, when Will McGirty realized what was happening. The cars, ready-loaded with pine ties, picked up speed down the track towards the fork junction where the points had been thrown. The line was open for Lima, Idaho Falls and beyond.

'They've kicked out the blocks,' McGirty yelled. 'Those loose cars'll never make it through the pass.'

By that time, Cargo and his men had already disappeared back into the early night. But it wasn't necessary for McGirty to know where to point the finger. He cursed long and hard as he pulled on his boots, then he drained a whiskey bottle and started across the hills for Whisper.

The runaway cars continued to gather speed. Within minutes they were travelling at forty miles an hour, threatening to derail at every curve through the descending hills. At each bend, a few more heavy ties scythed their way through the retaining chains, before being pitched from the flat-bedded cars.

With the wheel flanges screaming tight against the rails, the cars gathered speed. They met the fork and, without shunting up at the points, shot further down the southern

139

pass. As they sped onwards, touching sixty, the forward car's wheels came off the rails at the next bend it met. The rear car lifted and bucked into the front one, and with steel sparks showering the darkness, both went ploughing into a sheer, rocky wall. The flatcars crumpled into a pile of twisted iron, wheels and wood, the echoing crash reverberating madly through the rocky canyons of the Beaverheads.

Up at Blue Peak, Brady heard the crash, but mistook it for an explosion. He threw his saddle on his roan and with little consideration for his own or the roan's well-being, took to the down trail to Whisper.

The town was mostly in slumber when Brady raced up to Rown Vine's hotel. He ran to the back of the building and hammered on Clew's room door.

'What the...?' Clew started as he held the door open a few inches.

'There's hell to play in the canyon,' Brady stormed. 'I think there's been an explosion somewheres. Where's Jesse?'

'Right behind you, Brady,' Jesse replied. 'I heard you from way off. In these sort o' places, I ain't too trustin' of early bed times.'

'Get the engineer an' the fireman, Brady,'

Clew said. 'We'll meet you at the depot in fifteen minutes.'

'What's goin' on, Clew?' Jesse asked, as Brady went off to raise the engine crew.

'Don't know. But it ain't no fourth o' July party, that's for sure.'

21

Before the engine crew were located and got themselves to Whisper's rail depot, more than half an hour had passed. But the engineer, Liam Baird, was soon of the opinion that the explosion that Brady heard was a snow slide.

'It's the time o' year. Big build up hangin' on the side o' the mountain, lost its grip at last,' he suggested.

Brady shook his head. 'If you'd heard it, you wouldn't be sayin' that, believe me,' he replied spiritedly.

'Let's hope you're right,' Baird said. 'We can repair a few feet o' wrecked track, but we'd never plough our way through a canyon full o' snow.'

Brady had climbed aboard the engine's

tender. Clew and Jesse were about to follow when Will McGirty came panting up the track, waving his arms excitedly.

They all listened, their faces set with concern and anticipation as the ganger related what he'd seen.

'Sounds like you were right, kid,' Baird responded. 'Now we don't need to guess at what we'll find up there.'

'You're right,' Clew said. 'But we don't race off half-cocked. We got another car down here, so we'll load it with rails an' tools. You take charge o' that, Liam. If we work hard, we might he able to get goin' sometime after midnight.'

'We're goin' to need more men,' Baird said.

'I ain't seen much in town that quite fits that description,' Jesse replied drily. 'We'd best take 'em on up at the tie camp. If McGirty's boys can swing an axe, they can do the same with a goddamn sledge-hammer.'

It was in the early hours when they steamed out of Whisper. They pulled up to the tie camp with the engine's storm lantern cutting a bright path along the rails ahead of them. With McGirty's crew perched on the flatcar, Baird backed down to the junction and headed into the canyon. Running slow, and leaning from the cab, he groaned as he saw the ties that had been flung from either side of the two runaway cars. A half-mile on he slapped on the air, cursed as the big lantern revealed the rails and torn up rail bed. The flatcars had been reduced almost to kindling before plunging into the swift running creek that ran between trackside and the canyon wall.

Clew, Jesse and the others quickly jumped down to look things over.

'With a little sweat, we might have things opened up by daylight,' Baird observed. 'We'll toss everythin' into the creek.'

With a determination that wouldn't have been there if they hadn't owned that stretch of railroad, Clew and Jesse worked with Baird, McGirty, Brady and their fireman to clear the track. They worked by the light from the lantern, the fire-box and a couple of oil lamps. The sound of the creek's racing water filled their ears, and the forbidding walls of the canyon rose for several hundred feet above them. It was an eerie predicament, and wasn't entirely to Jesse's liking.

'This is costin' more'n a few dollars,' he grumbled, during a short breather. 'What are we goin' to do about it?'

'You mean *when*, Jesse.' Clew's voice was hard and flat as he answered his brother.

First light was streaking high above the canyon's rim before the new rails were laid and spiked. Clew ground his jaw at seeing the destruction of the cars, at how few of the ties could be dragged up as salvage.

'None of it's even much good for firewood,' the fireman observed.

'What *is* this all about, Clew?' Baird asked.

'Some of it's about Austen Rawfield ownin' a town, that he's goin' to call Rawfield. An' some of it's about a big railroad company gettin' even bigger. But all of it's about makin' gain at someone else's expense.' Clew was riled, and he angrily hurled a spike out into the creek. 'Hey, Jesse,' he called out. 'Remember it's my turn for takin' a swing at Max Cargo. An' you, Will, tell your boys to slip handles from their picks.'

'I might not bother with that, boss. Besides, most of 'em don't need pick handles. They got fists like Galway hams,' McGirty returned.

'Can you stay with the engine when we pull into the Peak?' Clew asked Baird. 'We know what cabins they're in, so we can try an' contain 'em.'

'They would've heard us go down the canyon, so they could be lyin' in wait,' Jesse warned.

'What use am I up on the footplate?' Baird asked Clew.

'After a few minutes I want you gettin' the whistle soundin' off like a banshee. An' you'll have Jesse keepin' you company.'

Jesse was quick to object, but Clew countered him.

'This little lady ain't more'n a rust box on wheels, but it's all we got,' he said. 'If it gets taken we'll all be in the deep an' treacly.'

The train backed up to Blue Peak, but the old engine couldn't turn a wheel without a squeal or clank or retching a noisy gobbet of steam. And thinking that Max Cargo and his men were unaware of what was about to happen was risky. But Clew had his plan, and he held to it. The band of assailants stood off from the doors of the two cabins, and Liam yanked long and hard on the whistle line.

But no one ran out, and Clew turned to Brady and McGirty. 'They're up to somethin'. They ain't at home, goddamn it. I wonder if Jesse was right?' he yelled.

With sudden foreboding the men turned to see Max Cargo and his timber markers advancing on them. They had been hiding in a run of nearby toolsheds, and now they rushed forward swinging a mixed collection of long-handled implements.

It gave them a momentary advantage, but McGirty and his wild Irishmen parried the initial onslaught. Within moments, men from both sides were felled, their faces and hands broken and bloody. A few of them managed to haul themselves back to their feet, but it wasn't long before they were down again. The exchange of blows was primal, and the fearsome sounds thumped and cracked across the camp.

Cargo seemed to know what was expected of him and he ran at Clew. But McGirty moved in and tripped him, neatly kicked the club from his hands. 'Come now,' the Irishman taunted, 'fight fairly, you big ape.'

22

For several minutes McGirty and Cargo slugged it out. They were toe to toe, but for all his toughness the ganger was getting the worst of it. Cargo flung a hard looping right, and his balled fist caught McGirty square on the jaw. The blow staggered him back three or four paces, before he doubled to the ground. Then Brady Rawfield shouted, and jumped in to take his place.

Cargo had a dark, crooked cut under his right eye that Jesse Brannin had put there previously. Brady opened it. He was fast and agile, moved around the timber marker, rocking him with sharp jabs to the left and right, but he couldn't put him down.

Clew saw the fight and wanted in. He had his back to a cabin wall while trading blows, but all he could do at the moment was throw fast, short jabs to keep his thick-set aggressor off balance. But suddenly the man changed his mind and came in with both arms flung wide. It was an obvious attempt at a bear hug, and Clew brought his right knee up. He connected with the man's lower belly and the air burst forth in a deep, agonized grunt.

Knowing he had a moment to assess the situation, Clew drew his fist back and level with the man's broad, flat face. 'Sorry, feller, but there's someone I just got to go meet,' he rasped, as he drove the punch in. The man's nose and mouth crumpled into a bloody mush, and he went over like the proverbial grain sack.

Busy as he was, Cargo had an eye for what was going on around him, an outcome. But although he was still on his feet, he could see the fight was going against him and his men. He'd had lost such fights before, survived to take on another one. It was why he was paid by Northern Pacific in the first place. So now, after already soaking up one beating, and with no real sense of loyalty to his men to hold him, he was ready to make an expedient exit.

Cargo saw Liam Baird leaning from the engine cab, but he failed to notice Jesse, who was flattened across the tender's cordwood fuel. To make a dash for the engine less than fifty yards away seemed possible, and how difficult could it be to operate a locomotive? Engineers didn't normally carry guns, so he could throw Baird from the cabin, just like they'd done to him. With the track repaired, he'd open the throttle and make off down the canyon, head straight for Lima or Idaho Falls, even Pocatello. In terms of his paymasters, he'd done what was expected of him. The destruction of material assets would cost the new owners several thousand dollars, give them a taster for what they could expect if they didn't come to heel. A few broken hand and head bones in a stick fight was of little consequence to most Northern Pacific officials.

Cargo made his decision and made a fast, dogged run for the engine. He'd got to within a few yards of the tracks, when Jesse raised himself on his haunches and fired two deliberate shots in front of him. The bullets were high and wide, but they turned Cargo. The man swung to the south, looked like he was taking to the canyon on foot. But another bullet soon kicked at the dust under his heels. Cargo stopped running and turned to confront Clew who was holding a .44 Colt steady in his hand.

'I wanted to use fists on you, Cargo, but due to one o' your mongrel bone-heads, my arm's begun to hurt real bad,' Clew snarled. 'So, for the time bein', get alongside the engine, with any others that's able to stand.'

'What we doin' with 'em?' Jesse yelled.

'Sendin' 'em down the canyon on the flat-car. Let 'em see how all them ties must've felt, eh? We'll ride the engine back to Whisper.'

Clew thanked the bruised McGirty and his tie-cutters for what they'd done. 'We'll send up the doc, together with a cash bonus. See if you can tidy up the place. From now on, it's all yours.'

'You ain't really sendin' 'em down the grade, are you?' McGirty asked with a painful smile.

'Naagh, waste of another flatcar. They're walkin'. An' if any of 'em turn back, kill 'em. That's an order.'

Max Cargo was weighing his chances against his crew. They knew that he'd have tried to run out on them, and he wondered how far he'd get before they ganged up on him, pitched him out into the creek.

'Get goin',' Jesse ordered. 'Remember this is my line. Don't ever meet me on it again.'

'We gave 'em hell, didn't we?' Baird said, as he tossed some cordwood into the engine's fire-box. 'Apart from losin' my fireman to a skull crack, I ain't had so much fun since watchin' Ma Harries's pig stompin' a rattler.'

Clew gave a jaded smile. 'But you still got to keep your eyes open,' he warned. 'Cargo an' his crew ain't the freshest eggs in the basket. They might not understand a heartfelt warnin'.'

At the telegraph office, Milly Matches was talking to John Shallote. He'd brought her news that the Brannins had left town in the early hours of the morning.

'An' young Brady was here,' he said. 'I reckon he must've gone up there with 'em.

150

Do *you* know what they're up to, Milly?'

Milly looked puzzled. 'I know they've tangled with Max Cargo. They wouldn't have taken the engine up there for that, would they?'

'I dunno, Milly. I'll find Butch Harries. Maybe we'll ride up there an' find out.'

Minutes later, Austen Rawfield arrived in a black temper. 'You an' your friends'll pay for this,' he fumed. 'I'll show you people what law means.'

'*I'm* the law in this town,' Shallote responded curtly. 'Wait till you know what you're talkin' about. Unless o' course, you *do know* what you're talkin' about.'

'What the hell do you mean?' Rawfield snapped.

'There was a time when folk headed for the fraidy hole when you barked, Austen, an' that included me. But not anymore,' Shallote said.

Rawfield stormed from the office and Shallote turned to Milly.

'Whatever it is, he'll be takin' it up with Clew and Jesse. I doubt if he'll be back to trouble you, Milly,' he said.

'Are you sure you know what you're doin', John?' Milly asked affectionately. 'It's his word that carries weight to get you elected.'

151

'That were *those* days, Milly. I'm thinkin' they're over.' The sheriff moved suddenly to the door and looked along the southbound track. 'It's them. They're back,' he said.

Milly followed Shallote outside, watched anxiously as Brady Rawfield leapt to the platform jetty. He shouted a greeting through the squeal and hiss of the braking engine; with hardly a glance, brushed past his father and ran to Milly.

'What *have* you been doin'?' Milly gasped seeing Brady's torn clothes, his dirt-streaked, bruised face.

'Hah, you should've seen the other guys, Milly,' the young Rawfield exclaimed proudly.

Milly listened as Brady told of what had occurred through the night and into the morning. The sheriff got a more explicit account from Clew and Jesse.

As was meant, Austen Rawfield was able to hear most of it, and eventually Clew turned on him.

'O' course *you* didn't know anythin' about *that*, did you, Mr Rawfield?' he mocked scornfully.

'If there's anythin' to be said, I'll say it in front of a court o' law, not *you*,' Rawfield shot back.

'Yeah, you might at that,' Clew said, and turned his back on the man.

'So what's goin' to happen next?' Milly wanted to know.

'Brady says there's an unused car lyin' idle at the end o' the Double R ranch sidin',' Clew said. 'That'll at least give us some operational provision. We're back in business an' lookin' for customers.'

For two days, Clew and Jesse made a round trip to Blue Peak. There were no further reprisals, and no sightings of Max Cargo or his men.

On the second day, they ran into a belt of rain that swept across the eastern slope of the Peak. It was the beginning of the late spring storms and would continue unabated for a week. The water filled the creeks and put much of the track sections under water. It was inevitable that train journeys to and from the Peak would be cancelled.

Liam Baird recruited a work force from McGirty's tie-cutters, and went to work clearing timber blowdown from the roadbed and replacing a number of unstable rails.

Jesse was summing up the situation and his thoughts. 'Our money's travellin' out a lot faster than it's comin' in, Clew,' he said.

'Yeah, I know. I would've pulled out before, had it only been your investment. But now *my* money's involved, we *stay*.'

'Hah. I thought you'd say that,' Jesse acknowledged. 'I just want a prod ... somethin' to let me know there's a reason behind what I got us into.'

And a few days later, there was. A cattle buyer from Idaho bought most of the Snake Plain calf crop. The tie-cutters sided the two flatcars with timber, made pens sound enough to transport the livestock to Pocatello.

'You heard anythin' more about that contract to supply ties to the Northern Pacific?' Clew asked Milly.

'Not yet. I hear McGirty's pilin' 'em up, though. You think word's out that I'm sidin' with the enemy?'

'No one's goin' to blame you for that, Milly,' Jesse chimed in. 'You should see Cargo's timber markers up close. Not that you ever would, o' course. First whiff of 'em, would stop you at twenty paces.'

Brady came in later and the four of them stood and jawed for a while.

'You should see the engine now,' Brady said. 'It ain't the same ol' chuff bucket that you boys bought. Baird's got himself a new

154

fireman, an' they done some paintin' an' polishin'. I'm goin' up to the Peak with 'em, why don't you come for the ride?'

Jesse suddenly looked as if he'd got something for his tribulations. 'As long's we ain't totin' firewood, just try an' stop us,' he said.

23

'She's a ripper all right,' Liam Baird said, as the engine pulled smoothly into the newly built reverse loop. 'Reckon on the way down, we'll top forty.'

Jesse was looking up at the northern flank of the Peak. 'What's that up there?' he asked, of no one in particular.

'I reckon it's the surveyors' base camp,' Clew answered. 'Looks like they got big campaign tents.'

'They must be lookin' at the route around the pass. The one that attorney said they'd make, instead o' blastin' a tunnel,' Jesse speculated.

'Yeah,' Clew agreed. 'The first chance we get, we're goin' up there to take a look. It'll take us a couple o' days, but we ought to know.'

On returning to Whisper, Milly greeted them with the news that Northern Pacific had made a request for freight cars. 'They're movin' up to the Peak with equipment an' a work crew.'

'Let's hope that's what it means,' Clew said. 'Did they say how many cars they need?'

'No. But I'd imagine they know how many, or how few we're left with. What do we do?'

'Looks like we'll have to use all o' both,' Jesse suggested with a brief smile.

Using four of their own freight cars, it took the Northern Pacific three days to move into Whisper and on up to Blue Peak. They carried mules, horses, scrapers, rails and tents. Together with a commissary car, upwards of a hundred men were sent to the rail head.

One of the workforce was Max Cargo. With apparent disregard to Jesse's threat, he had a new gang of hirelings with him. But they weren't of the same ilk as the timber markers.

'Hired guns, if ever we've seen 'em,' Clew said, dourly.

Jesse agreed. 'An' the livestock's for the scouts.'

The construction boss and his foremen were easily identifiable. They were experienced men, and under their direction and charge, a tented settlement quickly sprang up alongside the high running creek.

Milly's contract for the supply of ties had arrived, and McGirty had two carloads ready for delivery. Liam Baird got them pushed into the Blue Peak siding, and they all waited for instructions to move.

The following day, Brady asked Clew what he thought the hold up was about.

'Search me. I thought they were pressin' on with haste.'

'They'll be waitin' for a company director to arrive,' Milly suggested that evening. 'It's no small operation, even for Northern Pacific.'

'How many chiefs do they want?' Jesse asked.

'They want someone who can throw real weight around. Put the frighteners on people like us.'

'You got any ideas about 'em, Milly?'

'There's two: Isaac Belle an' Sam Stamper. They're the Montana names. Neither of 'em will have to send a cable for every sou that's spent or decision that's taken.'

Milly was right. Next morning, Sam Stamper arrived with his coterie of clerks, surveyors and engineers. The Blue Peak camp sprang to life, the surveyors from the high peaks returned and the first stakes were driven.

A team of drillers tackled prevailing outcrops of rock, the low booms of the blasting charges resounding down to the telegraph depot at Whisper.

'They're bluffin'',' Jesse said. 'They ain't goin' round the peak, spendin' hundreds o' thousands o' dollars, just to show they don't need us.'

'But they do, Jesse,' Clew responded. 'They can build around the pass, even go through it, but they ain't goin' down the goddamn canyon. That's where we are, an' where we're stayin'.'

Jesse shook his head with uncertainty. 'I still don't see their reasonin'. An' I reckon we were meant to find them document maps up at the Peak.'

'They think we'll submit to 'em, when the town gets killed off. There'll be nothin' for us, no customers an' no trade from the cow men. We'll sell up to 'em, what they wanted all along. But we ain't sellin', Jesse, an that's the trouble that's brewin'.'

Milly was leafing through the freight

158

transactions of the last few days. 'Made more money than we have in the last six months,' she said with mixed emotions.

'Yeah, but Clew reckons it's a deception,' Jesse observed wryly.

'At the moment, money's money, Jesse. I don't know whether it occurs to anyone else, but it's providin' us with an operational fund,' Milly said.

Sam Stamper arrived in Whisper the next day to arrange for supplies to be delivered to the Blue Peak camp. Clew and Jesse went to the mercantile to speak to Enoch Hudson about it.

'It's a slick trick, throwin' business our way ... gettin' us used to improved trade. But it ain't foolin' me like it should,' the store owner stressed.

'We all got to take what we can get,' Clew advised. 'They got to get their stuff from somewhere, so it might as well be you.'

'Yeah. Sooner or later, they'll be doin' business with us,' Jesse predicted. And the Brannins looked at each other with vaguely uneasy expressions.

That evening Clew and Jesse were sharing a bottle of whiskey with Enoch Hudson, when Milly ran into the store.

'Quick,' she gasped. Her face was drained of colour, and her shoulders heaved with anxiety. 'I went to the office to get some papers, an' saw a light from the siding. I went over to see Liam, but it wasn't *him*. There's someone else there ... two, I think. They're workin' on the engine. I couldn't see Liam.'

'Could you see what they were doin', Milly?' Clew asked, offering his glass.

'Not much. They were up in the cab.'

'Did they see you?' Hudson wanted to know.

'No, I don't think so.'

'Drink that, then go find the sheriff. Tell him to get over there,' Clew said.

'If it's Cargo's men, they'll be armed. You sure you want ol' Long John in on this?' Jesse asked, as he and his brother approached the rail siding.

'Yeah, it's his town, don't forget. We couldn't live with him if we didn't co-operate.'

'Engines is one thing, fellers, but Liam Baird's another,' John Shallote said, on joining them. 'We got to think of his well-bein' ... where he'll likely be.'

'OK, John,' Clew agreed. 'Any other ideas about how to play it?'

The sheriff nodded. 'Jesse, you stay back

160

an' keep us all covered. Clew, you get between me an' Jesse. I'll move in. I'm guessin' they ain't expectin' us.'

'Anythin' else?' Jesse asked.

'Yeah. If they don't do what we tell 'em, shoot 'em. Responsibility's all mine.'

Clew grinned with admiration. 'That's the Long John of legend. The one I was tellin' you about, Jesse,' he said.

The sheriff eased up the barrel of his single-barrel shotgun and took a few careful steps towards the engine. Clew covered him, and Jesse quietly edged around in a wide arc.

'You fellers on the engine,' Shallote called out. 'This is the sheriff, an' we just about got you surrounded.'

Immediately, one of the men kicked an oil lamp, and sent it flying from the cab. It crashed into the hard-packed dirt that edged the trackside and spurted a pool of dark oil. There was a few seconds before the oil caught, but most of it soaked into the ground and the flames were languid and blue.

'They're both up there,' Jesse yelled. 'Like fish in a barrel.' In the low dancing light, he saw a rifle barrel shoved in his direction, and he snapped off a quick, probing shot.

As Jesse's gunshot barked into the darkness, the sheriff was standing on the track at the rear of the tender, to the left of Jesse and Clew. The man with the rifle jumped from the footplate and turned to be confronted by him.

'I'd call it a day, feller,' Shallote said calmly and took a step forward. But the man ducked and threw himself sideways, ran into the surrounding dark. Shallote cursed and edged close to the deep shadow of the engine.

Now the second man swung down from the opposite side of the engine cab, on the far side away from Clew and Jesse. He saw the sheriff who was closing in, and he fired fast and instinctively.

The bullet took a chunk from the sheriff's left side, but he didn't go down. Still moving forward, he staggered against one of the engine's driving wheels. He saw the dark figure of his foe and pulled the trigger of his faithful shotgun.

An ounce of buckshot found its mark and smashed into the man's upper body. The blast lifted him from his feet, and he was dead before he hit the ground.

'We got a rat escapin' round here, Clew!' Jesse yelled.

The first gunman had run into the darkness beyond the low flaming oil, but he was headed straight between the .44 Colts of Jesse and Clew. Both of them shouted for the man to stop.

'Don't go any further,' Jesse added. 'I could miss you in this dark, hit you somewhere you wouldn't want me to. Just lie down an' don't move. Throw that rifle somewhere over here.'

'You OK, John?' Clew shouted as he ran to join the sheriff.

'Yeah. But I'm hurtin' more than this sinner,' the sheriff gasped. 'You go an' find Liam. He's here somewhere. Look in the toolshed.'

Clew found Liam Baird, trussed and gagged. He'd taken a blow to the head, and blood was oozing down the front of his face.

From the direction of the depot, Brady Rawfield suddenly shouted his presence. 'What's happened? You need any help?' he called out.

'Yeah. It looks like our engineer's taken a knock,' Clew answered back.

'I'm sorry,' Baird said. 'I heard 'em, but someone must've jumped me. I went into the real night. An' they stuck a goddamn oil wipe in my mouth. I'll never get rid o' the taste o' this.'

'There was two of 'em, an' we got both. Sheriff weren't quite so merciful as Jesse,'

Clew explained.

'I guess I'll never know which one of 'em lamped me,' Baird scowled painfully. 'Do you know who they are?'

'Cargo's men at a guess. We'll get a rig out here. Get you an' the sheriff to Doc Kelso.'

'I want Butch Harries down here pronto. He can deal with these loco thieves,' the sheriff was telling Jesse. 'He'd better bring a wagon.'

Baird and Jesse had a look at their engine. It was dark, but they made out two broken pipes that led to and from the throttle control. The damage was nothing that couldn't be repaired within an hour or so by a blacksmith, or as soon as Liam Baird was back in shape.

Clew questioned the captured gunman, but he got nothing. The man was tight-lipped, if not much else.

'Tap his head with a goddamn pick handle, until he tells you what you want to know,' Baird urged as he wavered to his feet. 'Or better still, crack his hands. He won't get back on anyone's payroll, then.'

24

Several days passed. According to the Missoula newspapers, work was proceeding beyond expectations in the tunnel north of the Peak. Of equal interest to Clew and Jesse was the news that Northern Pacific was building east from Jackson Ford. More freight was hauled up to the camp, and one evening a carload of labourers came up to boost Sam Stamper's workforce. It removed any lingering doubt that eventually there would be a showdown, and it would be south of Blue Peak. More than ever, Clew was anxious to see what work was being done up in the Beaverheads.

Liam Baird had only lost a couple of days, making light of the few stitches across the top of his head. John Shallote however, couldn't do more than shuffle ungainly down to his office.

'I never thought I'd see the day a single bullet would lay you up,' his deputy, Butch Harries, prodded him one morning. 'For years you been braggin' that you was as tough as any plains buffler.'

Brady Rawfield came up to the Peak with Baird one afternoon. It was the first time that Clew and Jesse had seen him in three days. 'Stamper's surveyin' crew are workin' a ways north already,' he reported. 'Cargo sends a man or two up with 'em each day. You'd think from that he's expectin' trouble up there.'

'Let's hope he keeps on thinkin' that,' Clew said. 'You be ready to pull out with us tomorrow mornin'. We can't wait any longer to get a look see. We'll leave early ... make it no more'n a three-day round trip.'

'Well, it's quiet enough at the moment,' Brady agreed. 'We can hit the high country above the Erskine Stock Pens. We can get up there without bein' seen.'

'Hey, fellers, I don't know if this means anythin' or not,' Jesse put in suddenly, 'but this mornin' I saw one o' their stew builders stripping the hide from a steer. I thought they was bringin' in dressed beef.'

'Er, they are, yeah,' Clew said. 'It's a big camp ... takes a lot o' meat to keep it goin'. Maybe they get the odd steer with hair. Why, what you thinkin'?'

'Maybe someone's supplyin' the camp with rustled beef? Max Cargo?'

'Hah, puttin' rustlin' alongside his other accomplishments now, eh?' Clew responded, none too seriously.

'Interestin',' Brady joined in. 'I don't know how long they could get away with a stunt like that. An' I ain't heard of anyone losin' stock. Dutch Barrow would know his tally to the nearest runt calf.'

'Yeah, but bear it in mind.'

'We will, Jesse,' Clew said. 'Meantime, we'll head up north. Just pack enough fixin's to get us there an' back. We'll travel as light as we can.'

They took a good breakfast at Rowan Vine's, were across Dutch Barrow's land and into the foothills by mid-morning. It wasn't long before the going became steeper, and they stopped several times to give their horses a blow. From their high perch, Snake Plain rolled into the distance below them.

'It sure takes the eye,' Jesse said appreciatively. 'Water, grass an' virgin timber. No wonder the Indians got snorty at being moved on.'

'Yeah, an' it's one o' their old trails we're hittin' on. An' no goddamn engineers' are ever goin' to best it,' Clew responded respectfully.

'You know, for the sake of a few goddamn

miles, that Northern Pacific could take in Whisper,' Brady said.

'But it's *them* few miles that's likely to cost 'em a fortune,' Clew replied. 'I told you, it's no use to 'em without our line.'

The halt was making Jesse restive. 'So how much further do you reckon it is, till we get to where we're goin'?' he wondered.

'Don't know exactly,' Clew answered him. 'But if we keep headed east, we'll get there. Soon, we can pull up for the night.'

Early next morning, they rode through a low, drifting ribbon of pungent smoke. Ten minutes later they came on an occupied prospector's shack.

'You're strangers,' the man croaked, drawing aside the sack from a window opening.

'There ain't goin' to be any foolin' you,' Jesse retorted.

'You lost or somethin'?' the man asked. He wasn't pleased at the company, and Clew warmed to him for it.

'You with them railroad fellers? The ones came over here a few weeks back?'

'Yeah, that's right,' Jesse agreed, for the sake of it. 'Huntin' critters ain't our speciality, so where'd we find 'em?'

'You won't. You may get to hear 'em, though. They're along the creek aways.'

As they moved off, Jesse twisted around in the saddle. 'What the hell are you burnin' in there?' he asked.

'Critters. An' I'm cookin' 'em,' the man said, and went back inside.

It was almost simultaneous with finding the creek, that the three riders heard the blasting.

'That ain't the sound of any creek diggin's,' Brady said, as they turned their horses closer to the water.

'Who are we meant to be?' Jesse asked Clew.

'Tie hacks, I guess.'

It wasn't long before they saw the preliminary stakes and rock piles that had been run across the pass. An hour later, a group of surveyors and rodmen gave them a friendly greeting.

'Good day to you,' one of them said 'You want to see Mose College. He's payin' top wages for almost any help he can get. You'll find him a mile or so upstream.'

'Thanks, we might do that,' Clew said, as they moved on.

They reached the site of the blasting and stood off a hundred yards watching, saw a deep cut being blown through a towering shoulder of rock. Strung out along a north-

ern slope of the Beaverheads, was a workforce that was two, maybe three times larger
than the one toiling at Blue Peak.

'The track's goin' through in another five
or six weeks,' Clew assessed.

'Yeah, I can see that. So what the hell's
goin' on at the Peak?' Jesse said.

'A big double-barrelled bluff, that's what.
They're goin' round the Peak all right, but
not from *there*. Why should they?'

'What do you mean?'

'Why should they invest millions in buildin', when there's already track there? *Our*
track. We turned 'em all down, but they'll be
back. An' this time it won't be for leisurely
consideration.'

'Jeez. Are you sayin' there's another fight
on?' Brady asked, with barely concealed
fervour.

'Yeah that's about it, young 'un. But it
won't be the finish of us,' Clew said, without
further explanation.

They spent the night east of the pass. Early
afternoon of the third day saw them moving
down from the foothills above Dutch Barrow's ranch. They were some miles distant
from the main house, when they saw a large
group of horsemen pull out and start riding
towards Whisper.

'What do you suppose is goin' on down there?' Jesse said. 'That's more'n Barrow's crew.'

Brady agreed. 'Albie Cave an' some o' *his* men must be with 'em,' he replied. 'Perhaps we should go an' find out.'

25

The sound of the approaching horses brought out Piggy Spade, an old stove-up 'puncher who did the odd jobs on Barrow's ranch.

'We saw Dutch hightailin' it to town,' Brady said. 'Who's he got with him, Piggy? What's wrong?'

'Him an' Albie Cave gone an' strung up one o' Rawfield's men.'

'Jeez. What the hell happened?'

'We been losin' beef, no secret in that. Last night they moved in on the Erskine Pens ... put their ropes on a couple o' fat yearlin's. There was a runnin' fight, an' one of 'em got caught. There's still range law out here ... we all know it.'

Clew shook his head, remembered what

Jesse had in mind. 'Obviously some of us forgot,' he said bitingly.

'We wanted to know what Cave an' Barrow were racin' into town for?' Jesse reminded Spade.

'They were goin' to see Rawfield. Sorry, Brady, your ol' man's gone too far this time,' Spade said.

'They've gone to *tell* him that, have they?' Clew asked impatiently.

Spade was still shrugging his shoulders when the three riders swung their horses onto the Whisper road.

Contrary to what Spade had said, Clew was thinking Jesse had got it right. The cattle stealing carried Max Cargo's hoofprints. He'd got others to do the work, that's what he was paid for.

The horses were deeply sweated when they swung into the town's main street. There was a suspenseful crowd of men and women gathered in front of the bank, which had already closed for the day. Propped up on crutches with his shotgun gripped tight in his right hand, John Shallote stood defiantly on the steps. Austen Rawfield was alone inside.

Clew, Jesse and Brady swung down from their saddles immediately they reached the bank's steps. Glass showered the footwalk where rocks and stones had been thrown at the building's front windows.

'Looks like a goddamn lynch party,' Jesse rasped.

'Yeah,' Clew agreed, 'somethin' we don't need.'

Albie Cave and Dutch Barrow shouldered forward menacingly. 'I didn't expect to see you boys linin' up against us,' Barrow spluttered angrily. 'Ain't the man done enough to you?'

'Sorry, feller, but *no*, he ain't done that much. He's doin' even *less* now,' Clew responded calmly. 'He failed to buy up the Growster-Matches line, don't forget.'

'He's been stealin' our stock from under our noses,' Cave said.

'You don't know that. In fact, how'd you know the rustlers' didn't run off some o' *his* beef?' Jesse snapped back.

'You already got trouble. If you're party to any *more* hangin's you'll get martial law out here, an' you wouldn't want that,' Clew said. 'You'll lose a lot more'n a few beeves, believe me,' he reasoned. 'Think about it, for Chris'sake. Get Rawfield to stop doin' the Northern Pacific's dirty work. Get him to work for *you*.'

'How'd we get him to do *that*? He never

has before,' Cave wanted to know.

'I don't know,' Clew answered back. 'Get him to put the title for his ranch in the name o' the town council, if there's one left. If he puts a foot wrong, you all take damages. It shouldn't be much more'n puttin' pen to paper. Enoch Hudson will know what to do.'

'That's young Brady's legacy, surely?'

'Put it in *his* name, then. It's the same thing. I'll just go an' make him the offer,' Clew suggested.

'You hear that, Rawfield? I'm comin' in. Shoot *me*, an' you'll live for about ten seconds,' he called out.

Clew pushed against the bank's big oak door and eased himself into the gloom. Austen Rawfield was sitting behind a large desk with a loaded shotgun in his hands. Sweat beading across his pale forehead told of the fear he was living with.

'You heard what my solution was for them outside, Rawfield. Tin-pot maybe, but it might save your hide.'

'Rubbish,' Rawfield snorted. 'I put a lot into the development o' that line. But you an' your brother put in everythin'. You're stretched to breakin' point, an' very soon you won't have a pot to piss in.'

'To the bunkered that's true, Rawfield.

But them that's more savvy, might start to wonder what our end game was.'

'Hah. You ain't even got a hand to play.'

'You got in too deep with the Northern Pacific. With us, you saw a skirmish, Rawfield, not a battle.'

'You got some sort o' triumphant option then?' Rawfield pushed.

'Maybe. How about if we turned our back on the trade that's movin' up north'? How about if we linked up with the south? We got a line down to Pocatello already. But another hundred miles or more, an' we'll be in Ogden. We'll be thinkin' Sacramento an' Chicago, not goddamn Missoula or Miles City.'

Rawfield ground his jaw in anxious confusion. 'Are you tellin' me that the Central Pacific's bank-rollin' you?'

'I ain't tellin' you anythin'. It's somethin' for you to spin over.' With a set-up placed, Clew backed off. 'Your son's outside,' he said. 'He don't think you had anythin' to do with stealin' cows, an' curiously enough, nor do I.'

'Yeah, well, right now that don't mean an awful lot,' Rawfield sneered. 'An' if you'd kept your acquisitive fingers off the pastries, we'd all of us be better off by now.'

'Well, I ain't agreein' with you on *that.*'

'I ain't askin' you to, goddamn it. An' I'll take care o' that deed.' Rawfield swung the barrel of his shotgun towards the half-open doorway. 'Get that ol' star-toter to break that mob up, an' arrest 'em. They're formin' a goddamn lynch party.'

'Yeah, it looks like there's some chickens come home to roost. That's the price o' bein' *you,* Rawfield. I already been reminded there's range law still operatin' in these parts.'

The crowd stayed to hear what transpired, but remained unconvinced that the show was over. Cave and Barrow chose to regard the outcome as a personal victory.

John Shallote flicked at shards of broken glass with the end of his crutch and sat down on the top step. 'I been standin' there for nearly an hour,' he muttered wearily.

'Where's that deputy o' yours?' Jesse asked.

'It was quiet, so I told him to take off for a few hours. Huh, shows my grasp o' the situation, eh? Reckon I'll have to send him up to the Erskine Pens when he gets back.'

Brady shuffled his feet uneasily. 'My pa must be weakenin',' he suggested to Clew.

'Seein' sense is strength, a sort of investment, Brady,' Clew responded. 'But let's hope there's a moment o' weakness when he reports to the Northern Pacific,' he added, with a scheming smile.

26

The next day was Sunday, and Whisper was quieter than usual. Clew and Jesse were sitting talking out front of Vine's, when Liam Baird walked up.

'Brady ain't around, is he?' he said, and Clew and Jesse shook their heads.

'Good. It's just that earlier, I saw his pa taking a rig out. Looked to me like he was headed for Blue Peak. After what happened here yesterday, you'd think he'd be a bit more careful o' who he was mixin' with.'

'You would normally, yeah,' Clew agreed. 'But he's got an appointment to keep ... an important message that needs deliverin' to Sam Stamper.'

'How do you know? What sort o' message?' Baird asked.

Jesse was about to ask his brother the same question, when Rowan Vine came out and asked them in for dinner. 'Sunday

177

Special boys. Comb your hair, an' kick the dirt from your boots,' she said.

It wasn't until they were alone later in the afternoon that Jesse was able to ask Clew about the appointment that Austen Rawfield had to keep.

'I'd have got around to tellin' you, Jesse.'

'Says you. What's it all about? You know somethin' I don't?'

'I know what I've *done*. It occurred to me while I was lookin' over one o' Milly's maps,' Clew started to explain, saw that he held Jesse's interest. 'You know how the Union an' Northern Pacific ain't exactly bed fellows?'

'Yeah, I know that, Clew. Go on.'

'Well, it got me to thinkin'. What would happen if the *Union* company got interested in makin' us an offer? Buildin' through Snake Plain to meet us outside o' Whisper? A new line straight up from Idaho Falls? Strange thing is, it ain't so far-fetched. Can you imagine that, Jesse?'

'I can imagine it, Brother. But at the moment, that's about all. An' *that's* what you'd have Rawfield believe? *That's* what you let him in on?'

'Yeah.'

'How the hell are you goin' to make it

178

work beyond what you made up already?'

'Let the word out. They say a lie can travel a mile while truth's puttin' its boots on. An idea, together with them two companies' mistrust of each other, should be all we need.'

'So when?' Jesse asked.

'Not just yet. If I've got some explainin' to do, I don't want Milly gettin' wind of it.'

Supplies had been steadily arriving in Whisper. They were to augment the dwindling stores up at Blue Peak and the work-forces in the near Beaverheads.

'At least they'll have to *buy* their meat now,' Shallote remarked sarcastically. Having left his crutch behind, he was feeling and walking better. 'Somethin' else worth mentionin', Clew,' he said. 'As I was passin' the bank, Rawfield asked me what I'd heard about the Union Pacific showin' interest in your set-up.'

'What did you say?'

'The truth. That I'd never heard the like. Why, have you?'

Clew shook his head. 'Naagh. Who but the Northern would be interested in us? Can't think where he got that idea from, John.'

Later on in the day, Liam Baird came to

see them again, this time with more serious news.

'What's up now?' Jesse smiled openly.

'Somethin' or nothin'. I've seen where they're goin' to blast,' he started off. 'There's goin' to be a road bed high above the creek. It ain't nothin' more'n a goat ledge, but it's been marked out.'

'That'll cost 'em millions,' Jesse said disbelievingly. 'An' take 'em a year.'

'It's much more significant,' Baird added.

'How do you mean, *more significant?*' Clew asked him.

'The waste rock. When it's blown, they ain't goin' to freight it down here, all neat an' tidy. They'll tip it straight into the canyon. It'll hit the floor somewhere along the rail bed. That means the creek's goin' to rise an' the tracks'll subside. There'll be nothin' left o' your rail line after the first couple o' blastin's.'

'Well, it solves the problem o' where our fight's goin' to be,' Jesse figured. 'One less thing to worry about, eh?'

Clew nodded. 'If Stamper don't come to see us in the mornin', I'll go an' see *him,*' he said thoughtfully.

Sam Stamper arrived in Whisper shortly after nine the next day. He was there primarily to see Clew and Jesse, but he made believe other business and spent some time with Austen Rawfield. It was pushing noon when he walked into the rail depot.

For a while Clew had been alone in the office. Jesse had ridden up to the canyon with Brady to see for themselves what was going on.

'Mr Brannin? I'm Sam Stamper,' his visitor announced with customary authority.

'Yeah, I know who you are,' Clew returned, and indicated that Stamper take a seat. 'What can I do for you?' he asked.

'An interestin' start,' Stamper granted. 'But it's more what *I* can do for *you*. We're explorin' the possibilities of goin' around the wall o' the canyon, in case you didn't know. We think it's a feasible move, but an expensive one.'

'Very,' Clew acknowledged, but offered nothing more. It was a draw tactic that he'd often used to elicit information from clients.

'Yes. Well, I know that Noel Alliss made you an offer, several offers, as did Royston Brough, for your part o' the railroad known as the Growster-Matches Link.'

Clew nodded non-committally, waited for Stamper to continue.

'Alliss's best offer was fifty thousand, I believe?'

Clew nodded again. 'If you say so.'

'I *do*, Mr Brannin. An' now I'm wonderin' if you don't regard that sort o' money as quite so triflin' any more. Particularly if I said I'd double it.'

Clew gave a thin, cold smile. 'Brough, Alliss, Rawfield, you an' the Northern Pacific,' he cited. 'I reckon we got ourselves a gold strike, an' you got the colic for it.'

'That's right, Mr Brannin, an' that's why we're now offerin' one hundred thousand dollars. What was bein' sold as scrap is now worth a fortune. You hit pay dirt, an' I ain't makin' out otherwise.'

'Yeah, I know. But as I told Alliss, it really ain't the money. It's the town, an' a lot o' the folk who go with it. You come from a hard bitten world, Mr Stamper, but unless you're prepared to bring Whisper into your reckonin', there'll never be any sort o' deal, an' that's my last word.'

Stamper thought for a moment, then nodded at Clew's line of reasoning. 'If you think you're goin' to haul this flea-bit, end town into the rest o' the world, Brannin, forget it,' he said testily. 'You'll never last that long.' Stamper pushed himself from the chair and stood in the doorway. 'I ain't come off second best before, an' I don't intend to start now. You're small fishes, an' you're goin' to get fried,' he threatened.

Clew fixed the railroad executive with an unforgiving stare. 'If you mean to blow rock off the west wall an' fill our road bed, *post a guard*,' he rasped. An' don't sleep too soundly or take a lone walk, 'cause *I* don't aim to come off second best either.'

27

Clew didn't tell Milly Matches everything that had passed between Sam Stamper and himself. But she already knew there was some sort of confrontation looming.

'Isn't that closin' the door on any further discussion?' she asked, after thinking over what he *had* said.

'Yes, ma'am, it sure does look that way,' he said wryly. 'I'm going to spend the rest o' this day out on the Plain. A few weeks ago, Cave an' Pepper an' most o' the others out there were ready to put 'emselves on the line ... for them an' us. The rustlin', such as it was, has been put down, but that trouble at the bank might have taken the edge off their enthusiasm. I've got to go an' find out. Can you tell Jesse an' Brady that me an' Stamper had a talk? They'll most likely be here before I get back, so we'll meet up later.'

Aside from Dutch Barrow, Clew found that the Snake Plain cowmen were just as ready to throw themselves into the upcoming fight, as they had been before.

'Leave Dutch to us,' Albie Cave told him. 'He can be a stubborn ol' mule, but nothin' we ain't seen before. He knows the way you handled Rawfield was the right one. He just needs us to tell him again.'

When Clew got back to town, it was full dark. Jesse and Brady were waiting for him at Vine's Hotel.

'Before you start firin' off at me,' he said, 'tell me what happened along the canyon.'

'The surveyors was crawlin' all over the place.' Jesse began to give details. 'One o' the foremen had a gang workin' on the slope. Next, they'll be draggin' equipment up it. An' Cargo was there with his gang. I'm tellin' you, Clew, the sooner we get up there onto the rim, the better off we'll be. The Lord never helped a man who sat on his ass an' waited.'

'Well, I wasn't exactly lookin' for *His* help, Jesse, though I discovered we still got most o' the *ranchers* on our side. But I'm not goin' to send anyone lookin' for a bullet, till Stamper actually starts blastin' rock down on us.'

'That won't be long,' Jesse pronounced. 'Don't be too surprised if sometime before nightfall tomorrow, Liam can't make it through the canyon.'

Clew thought for a moment before responding. 'Then the three of us will take a ride up there after our mornin' train pulls out,' he decided. 'We'll head for the junction. If needs be, stay there until we know one way or another.'

When Brady had left them, Jesse asked for an account of Stamper's visit, other than Milly had been able to tell him. Clew gave him the fact and detail.

'An' did that Union Pacific windy o' yours rattle him?' Jesse asked.

Clew smiled thinly. 'Yeah, o' course it did. If a Union agent showed up here tomorrow, he'd up sticks an' go home.'

When Liam Baird ran the engine and one flatcar into Blue Peak next morning, upwards of a hundred workers were bolstering the track on which Stamper intended to haul plant machinery up the west wall. The route it was to take was clearly indicated.

'They'll never haul a goddamn train up *that* grade,' Baird insisted. 'Not unless they're usin' some sort o' cableworkin'.'

Cargo and his gunmen were in evidence, but they did little more than move with the sun.

'Do you reckon Stamper's workin' on his defence plans?'

'Yeah. It's probably why he's usin' one o' them campaign tents,' was Clew's wry suggestion.

Blasting carried on during the afternoon, and they used the rock as trackside fill. At first dark, the men returned to camp with the teamsters and mules.

It was the end of a long, wearisome day of inaction. 'They'll soon make it to the ledge,' Jesse remarked in between yawns. 'I'm reminded o' that imaginary Union agent you were talkin' about, Clew. It would sure throw Stamper an' his cohorts into a blue funk if one of 'em turned up now.

'Many a true word, Jesse,' Clew said. 'Given that, if one of 'em gets sight of a Missoula newspaper, they just might.'

As Jesse predicted, Sam Stamper's drillers and rock blasters attacked the west wall shortly after noon the following day. As soon as the first string of bore holes was completed, charges were rapidly placed and exploded. The earth rumbled and tons of rock sheared from the wall, went into a sliding fall to the creek below. The debris packed the road bed, then bounced and rolled to the fast-running water alongside the track.

'Is that enough for you?' Jesse spoke angrily, from their vantage point at the junction. 'Or would you like to be underneath it, before makin' your *final* decision?' he added with spleen.

'Yeah, that's more than enough, Jesse,' Clew responded flatly. 'An' they're goin' to send down a lot more rock before the day's over. We won't even be able to cow-catch it out o' the way.'

Jesse stared at him aghast. 'Or get killed tryin'. That's what'll happen if we're down there when they blast off some more goddamn mountainside.'

'I reckon it's time to put up,' Clew decided.

'I'd like to be up there on the rim with a rifle. I'd give 'em a headache they wouldn't recover from,' Jesse threatened.

Liam Baird leaned from the footplate and took a long look down the canyon. He cursed, turned to face Clew and Jesse.

'It'll be a miracle if them rocks ain't ruptured the road bed. Like I said, the creek level's goin' to build, an' if they keep blastin', it won't be long before the whole canyon's a water race.'

Stamper's drills were soon biting into the west wall again, and a half-hour later, another string of dynamite was detonated. Once again, rock flooded down into the creek, blanketing the rail bed. Up on the ledge, men swarmed back to work as soon as the wind blew the thick acrid dust clear of the site. Using long-handled crowbars, they prized off great pieces of fractured rock, toppled them down to the canyon floor.

Clew was thinking fast. But he didn't waver in his initial resolve of retaining a line from Blue Peak through to Idaho Falls. He shielded his eyes from billowing curl of dust and smoke and looked to the ledge. 'Today's your turn, tomorrow it's mine,' he said with compelling menace.

'You've said that once or twice before, Clew. Got any significance, has it?' Jesse asked, his intolerance of the situation getting ever clearer.

'Now we got somethin' to act on. Before, there was only the threat,' Clew responded. 'That would have been unlawful an' preventative. Now we'll dispense the goddam legal cure, so help me. We start by goin' back to Whisper.'

28

Clew and Jesse were just mopping up the gravy of Rowan Vine's night-time fixings when Austen Rawfield paid a visit to the small dining-room. But his blustering manner and flinty expression was now more rueful.

'I figure it's a man's right to make money when an' where he can, an' I make no apologies for it,' he began. 'But some things are happenin' that's got me to thinkin' maybe there's one or two other things as well. I've come to tell you that I ain't part o' what's happenin' up at Blue Peak.'

Jesse looked up at Rawfield. 'If one o' them other things you got to thinkin' about's how to stay alive, Rawfield, you best stay right here,' he said unsympathetically. 'That ledge ain't the only place that fuses are goin' to get lit. With your reputation, an' the way you been sidin', this ain't a good time for you to be abroad.'

'You might as well know, if you don't already, that your boy's with us,' Clew added. 'We're all done talkin' money with Mr Stamper, an' at midnight, we're ridin' to let him know.'

'Is Brady goin' to the ranch to recruit some o' my men?' Rawfield asked.

Clew shook his head. 'I don't think so. We don't need 'em.'

'If you do, they're loyal. If you get word to 'em, they'll listen to Brady.'

'We'll try, Mr Rawfield. Meantime, you stay here. Use one of our rooms, an' keep the door locked. If anyone comes knockin', they won't be in the mood for any long or short-winded explanations, or pardons.'

An hour later Clew and Jesse had their horses saddled. They were thinking about their meeting, when John Shallote walked through the barn doors.

'Hold up, boys, I want to talk to you,' he hailed.

'Yeah, thought you might. There's some meetin's you need, an' some you don't,' Clew muttered.

The sheriff heard him. 'Yeah, that's right,' he countered. 'Now I'm goin' to tell you boys somethin'. Stamper's got men here in town,

190

an' they know what you got in mind. It's the same as I already know, you chuckle-head.'

'We ain't tried to keep it a secret, Sheriff,' Jesse said. 'It's just that–'

'Just that you thought I was past it,' the sheriff cut in. 'Well, I'm ridin' to the west wall with you, an' *I'm* givin' the ultimatum to Stamper. That's in *his* interest. What's in *yours*, is it's an *ultimatum*. If they don't comply, we exchange lead,' Shallote assured them with an authority of office. 'That's another way of sayin', I'm backin' your play.'

'That's good, John,' Clew granted. 'We're goin' to have thirty or so men on the Plain between now an' midnight.'

'Then you've *all* got to remember what I said.'

Clew nodded. 'Yeah, an' that's all right with us. We'd rather have you an' the law out front, than shootin' from behind.'

It was shortly after midnight when the sheriff led his small army across the north corner of Snake Plain and up into the foothills of the Beaverhead Mountains. He was aiming to cut through the hills above the tie camp, to attain a ridge some distance below the scene of Sam Stamper's blasting operations.

'Let's hope there's some good cover up

there,' Jesse said.

'There will be. Where the caps are criss-crossed, you get deep fissures. A man can crawl through without bein' spotted. We'll be leavin' the horses in the timber.'

Brady Rawfield had four of his father's men riding with them. They were hardened ranch hands, but knew how to use firearms. Two of them, Wilf Bascoe and Cromer Watts, had schooled Brady in most of what he knew.

The night was still and bright, the moon so late in its rise that men and horses cast their shadows ahead and couldn't overhaul them. The drone of low voices mingled with the sound of horses snorting, the creak and grind of leather and riding gear.

There was much talk of Austen Rawfield. Dutch Barrow insisted it could be a grave mistake to believe there was any kind of rift between Rawfield and the Northern Pacific. But Cousin Pepper and some of the others thought differently.

'Christ, you can hear Barrow's take, back in Whisper,' Jesse protested.

'Don't let it bother you,' Clew said. 'There's no way we're goin' to surprise that crowd. Stamper knew the score the moment he started blastin'. I'll be surprised if right this moment, every man up there ain't armed to the teeth.'

The low foothills had been felled of timber long ago, were now mantled with near impenetrable scrub.

'You should o' traded them mounts for a couple o' brush poppers,' Brady observed, as he watched Jesse heel his mare through a scratchy thicket.

But eventually the riders left the valley floor and began to climb. With Shallote taking point, they stretched out in single file, and in less than an hour, reached new timber and relatively easy going.

Jesse judged that now they were above and beyond the tie camp – 'McGirty's there alright,' he said. 'But he's usin' his head – there ain't a light to be seen. I wonder how he explained to his crew that they ain't in on the fight?'

'Huh, neither are *we* yet,' Clew countered. 'The night's real young, Jesse.'

The trail John Shallote was taking began to take them off to the east, where the timber thinned. They were approaching the canyon's rim, but it was another thirty minutes before the sheriff called a halt. He wanted the horses left where the timber broke, and two men assigned to guard them. Then he called all the men around him.

'Before we start workin' up the rim, there's a thing or two I want to say,' he addressed them sternly. 'The sun's startin' to get up early, an' in less than an hour we'll be seein' what we're up against. I warned you all before we set out, an' I'm tellin' you again, there's to be no shootin' unless I tell you.'

'He's talkin' to you, Dutch,' one of Albie Cave's 'punchers taunted.

'I'm talkin' to every last one o' you god-damn cow prodders,' Shallote rasped in reply. 'If any o' them railroaders has dug in on that west wall, I'll give 'em a chance to clear out. But if they won't go, an' peaceably, *then* we get tough with 'em.'

'I reckon they'll be pissin' on us before you're convinced o' their intentions,' Jesse objected. His belligerent viewpoint won the muttered support of the Snake Plain men, but the sheriff bristled.

'I *always* want to be convinced, Jesse. It's one o' the ways to get to be an old man,' he growled.

'OK. but we don't have to sit here twiddlin' our thumbs till dawn, to find out what we're up against,' Clew declared. 'I don't think my nerves'll take it. Why don't I go an' scout this rim?'

194

'Good idea, an' I'll go with you,' Cousin Pepper said. 'That's if the sheriff ain't got an objection.'

Clew was certain they'd find Stamper's men dug in along the rim, and doubtless alongside Max Cargo's gunhands. Shallote's notion of parleyin' with them was more like wishful thinking.

The old sheriff then surprised both men. 'I'm taggin' along,' he told them. 'Havin' got this far, I don't aim to miss anythin'.'

Clew turned to Jesse. 'I'm your brother, don't forget. So you hear one shot fired, an' you come runnin' with the rest o' your god-damn army, you hear.'

29

Clew made his way to the lip of the rim. Far below, he could see the creek running white, almost fluorescent, between the sheer walls of the canyon. 'Remember, if there's any-thin' movin' ahead, it ain't critters,' he said quietly. 'They moved out some time ago.' He waited then, until Cousin Pepper had positioned himself to the left, and John

Shallote was working along between them.

By taking advantage of every rise and fall of rock, every clump of scrub pine, they moved along the rim for nearly 200 yards without any sighting or sign of movement. Then, without warning, a rifle cracked out from the lip of the rim. It was far ahead of Clew, but the bullet ricocheted and whined over his head. He sucked air through his teeth, flattened out against the rocky floor, as a second shot pinged off the rocks and zipped into the darkness.

Cousin Pepper had caught the second muzzle flash as he crawled around an outcrop. He flung his rifle to his shoulder and fired off four rapid shots at where, for a spilt second, the night had sparked red. Immediately, bullets began to sting the rocks around him, the sound as ferocious and scary as that of a tormented hornets' nest.

'We found 'em,' he shouted, as Clew and John Shallote made their way towards him warily. 'That could put your mind at rest, Sheriff,' he dashed out keenly. 'They're spoilin' for a fight, an' they ain't about to listen to any o' your official jawbone.'

'They don't know who the hell's up here,' Shallote returned just as huffily. 'But come sun up, I'll let 'em know. Now, we best drop back before the rest of us get our pants shot off. Whoever that is out there, they've got the eyes of a goddamn hootie.'

Clew led the way back the way they'd come, and within minutes they met the rest of the posse. Now that he knew where the enemy was lodged, Shallote proposed quitting the rim and, in the few minutes of remaining darkness, moving to the fringe of the timber. It was a position that would command the newly built road up the west wall of the canyon.

It didn't take them long, and wasn't without bursts of gunfire from out on the rim – wild, bugbear shots that startled, but found no mark.

'They know it's us, for Chris'sakes. Who else could it be? An' now they know we're gettin' set for tomorrow. They're just tryin' to pinpoint us,' Jesse muttered, as he hunkered behind a stand of recently felled pine, with Clew, Brady and half-a-dozen others.

'Well, they'll be sorry when they find out,' Clew said. 'From here, we can keep 'em from usin' the road, an' we're still high enough to break up anythin' they got in mind on the rim.'

The tips of the eastern peaks glowed pink in the early light of dawn and, as the sun climbed, it revealed the preparations that Sam Stamper's men had made for battle. On the rim itself they had gathered up loose rock and erected a series of low barricades. Clew thought it was from about where the shots had been fired at him and Cousin Pepper, but how many men were there, was anybody's guess. No one was to be seen on the road. But wherever they looked along the line, they all saw the glint of sunlight on rifle barrels.

'Well, you said they'd all be armed, Clew,' Jesse said sternly. 'Lord knows what kind o' gunhands his pick an' shovel men are makin', but it's a sure bet they won't be pushed off their hill without a fight.'

'Can you see that, John?' Clew asked, as the sheriff moved alongside them. 'They got guns bristlin' like the back of a nervy porcupine.'

'Yeah, maybe I have given 'em enough rope, eh boys?' Shallote gave a small, weary smile. 'You got us a plan B?'

Clew turned and rested his back against the pine. 'Cousin an' his men can stay here an' make the place look sort o' lived in. The rest of us'll drop down to the bottom o' the slope and go after them birds from the creek side. We could throw lead at 'em all day from here, without smokin' 'em out.'

'They've got us well outnumbered,' the sheriff commented, knowing that nothing would be gained from staying where they were. 'We'll be fightin' uphill, an' that ain't somethin' I'd normally recommend.'

Jesse grinned. 'An' fightin' on your own cosy little terms is somethin' else you don't get old on, Sheriff. Let's just give it a try,' he said defiantly.

'Or die in the goddamn attempt eh?' Shallote grinned back.

30

It took the men an hour to work down through the trees and get across the tie spur. Whoever was giving the orders to Stamper's men, speculated on the move and wasted valuable amounts of ammunition in attempting to divert or hold them.

When the advance party broke through to the creek, there was a mad scramble up on the slope where Stamper had stationed more than fifty armed workmen. They were there to guard the approach to the ledge and the rim above, but now, caught from the rear, they were on the wrong side of their cover. The men from the Plain's ranches didn't wait for any word from their sheriff and studded the side of the road with a fusillade from their assortment of Colts, carbines and rifles.

'There's a couple o' gents who won't be attendin' this week's prayer meetin',' the sheriff said brusquely.

'An' there'll be a few more when Pepper opens up on 'em,' Jesse yelled back.

In scuttling to find shelter from the line of fire from below, the defenders had left themselves open to attack from Cousin Pepper and his men in the timber. All they could do was kick up a low barricade of scree and rock and grub down behind it. As safe as they could be, they started to return Shallote and his mens' gunfire.

During a lull in the fighting, John Shallote discussed a new tactic with Jesse, Clew and Dutch Barrow.

'We can push 'em back up the slope if we go at 'em Injun fashion,' he claimed.

'That's somethin' we rarely do in our line o' work, Sheriff,' Clew said.

'Yeah,' Jesse agreed. 'What the hell's Injun fashion?'

'Pick your cover an' move towards it in short bursts,' Shallote said with conviction. 'It's the only way we're gettin' anywhere near 'em.' He sent a man to inform Cousin Pepper of their intended move. 'An' you tell that crazy son-of-a-bitch to be careful with his rifle, or he'll be cuttin' *us* down.'

The sheriff's strategy went well for a time and the fight moved a third of the way up the slope. From the rim, Max Cargo and his gunmen laid down a steady barrage of fire, but they found no target.

Jesse crawled up beside Clew. 'I ain't goin' any further, Clew,' he rasped, breathless and jittery. 'This time we really are between a rock an' a hard place. Look ahead. There ain't so much as a goddamn pile o' bear crap for the next fifty yards.'

Clew carefully scanned the way ahead. Stamper's men were now in position to resist any further advance, let alone attack.

'Jesse's right. We'll be cut to pieces if we keep this up, John,' he said. 'Give me an hour with three or four men, an' I'll get up on the rim of the east wall. There's no other way to get the better o' this fight.'

'What makes you think you can get up there?' the old sheriff snapped.

'Brady says he knows a way. We can either

go through 'em, or skip past 'em.'

The sheriff thought it over for a few moments. 'OK,' he decided. 'Who you takin'?'

'Jesse, Brady, an' a couple of his boys... Bascoe an' Watts ... someone to look out for the horses. But you keep shootin', John. Don't let that bunch get the idea we've changed our mind about stormin' the slope.'

To reach the east wall, Brady led them north back through the timberline. Then, they swung out to Snake Plain to avoid the camp or any trail ambush. They arrived at Blue Peak and pressed forward, made the climb unopposed to where they hitched their mounts in to the trees.

'We should make short work o' this,' Jesse rapped as, fifteen minutes later, they walked along the high rim. 'This is how *they* must've felt, when they thought they had *us* penned.'

'Yeah, but *we* knew they were there,' Brady said, glancing at Clew.

'That's right,' Clew confirmed. 'Shall we introduce ourselves?'

Max Cargo and his gunmen were stretched out at the head of the slope firing an occasional shot down at the sheriff and his men. Jesse's first bullet was wide, but the spit of rock shale it kicked up had an urgent, bracing effect.

Cargo swore, raised himself on an elbow, and stared at the opposite rim. As usual, his personal safety came first, but he wasn't gutless. He knew it was fatal to remain where he was, that the fight was over, unless whoever was on the east rim was quickly driven off.

Shouting sharp orders at his men, he leaped to his feet. Big man though he was, he outdistanced most of them in his run for the timber.

From the rim, Cromer Watts raised the tip of his rifle after making a hit. 'There's one didn't make it,' he growled almost ruefully. 'I guess he'd've done the same to me.'

'An' got paid for doin' it,' Jesse reminded him.

Then they noticed a second man staggering towards safety.

'Let him be,' Clew said. 'I reckon there's one or two more hurtin' just as bad.'

Before the wranglers who were guarding the sheriff's string of horses knew what was happening, Cargo and his men had overwhelmed them. They took the mounts they needed and, leaving their own wounded men to fend for themselves, were soon running downgrade. Fifteen minutes later, they stepped across the rail tracks beneath the shadow of Blue Peak. There was no reason for them to avoid the camp, and they raced through, kicked on towards the higher ground.

Unaware of what was happening, Clew and Jesse turned their attention to the slope. Stamper's men, now caught front and rear, hesitated. Shortly, one man threw his gun away and another two followed. Four, then five and six stood up, moved forward with their hands raised. It was the beginning of the end, and in a few minutes their fighting was done.

From their perch on the east rim, Clew and the others saw their colleagues disarming the construction crew and driving them back to camp.

'If ol' John can only hold up for a few days, I'll wager, the goddamn Northern Pacific will meet our terms,' Clew said.

'An' if we were to let the Union in as an option?' Jesse suggested.

'It's worth a thought,' Clew admitted. 'But three or four days should give us time enough either way.'

31

Clew and the others were sitting their saddles when they noticed a moving column of woodsmoke from the direction of Whisper.

'Hah, no mystery about what's burnin' there,' Jesse exclaimed. 'It's Liam with our own little iron horse. But I thought you told him to keep out o' this?'

'I did,' Clew grinned. 'His curiosity got the better of him, I guess. Not to mention a vested interest, some professional pride, maybe?'

They caught sight of their locomotive when Liam Baird ran it to within a hundred yards of the junction and stopped. A dozen armed men jumped down from the tender and cab.

'There's your reinforcements, Clew,' Wilf Bascoe remarked with a wry smile. 'Timin' ain't perfect, though.'

'It *is*,' Clew said. 'The sheriff can use 'em. He's goin' to have to arrange some back up. We can run clothes, blankets an' fixin's up to him ... anythin' they need.'

Unsuspecting of any new danger, the men began moving down the trail. Jesse ranged ahead, and although he was weary and hungry, it was characteristic of him to remain vigilant when riding. It saved them now, for if he'd been sleeping in the saddle, he wouldn't have heard the soft rumble of running horses. The moment the sounds broke into his awareness, he drew rein and threw up a hand.

'We've got company. Everyone off the trail,' he rasped. He stood in the stirrups and peered down the mountain. 'It's Cargo's bunch. Six of 'em, an' they'll be pilin' into us within minutes.'

'Let 'em come,' Clew said calmly. 'They'll be close, so no rifles. Use your belt pistols,' he advised.

The ominous quiet from across the creek hadn't gone unnoticed by Cargo or his riders. They all took it to mean the fighting was over, and that it had gone badly for their chosen paymasters. When some of them suggested they turn back, Cargo wouldn't listen. He'd fared badly by the Brannins, particularly at the hands and fists of Jesse, and it had left him with a personal score to settle. The chance of finding Clew and Jesse among those on the east rim was enough to drive him on.

The trail grew steeper, slowed their ascent. Ten minutes on, and they stopped to give the horses a blow. Cargo raised his head and stared warily around him, cursed vehemently when Clew Brannin appeared from the pines ahead.

Immediately they were being pinched from both sides, and Cargo was looking directly down the barrel of Clew's .44 Colt.

'Stick up your hands,' Clew droned.

The two riders either side of Cargo broke away and plunged down the trail in reckless flight. Jesse and Cromer Watts stepped their horses forward and blocked anyone else from heading in the same direction. The other Cargo men held their ground, but they dropped their reins and held up their hands in acceptance of defeat.

For a short moment, Cargo locked eyes with Clew, then he saw the cold scorn on Jesse's face. His frustration and anger got the better of him, and he made a despairing grab for his gun. He drew and fired, but it was too fast and unfocused.

The wild, hurried shot didn't come within a yard of Jesse, but in missing him, the bullet tore into Brady Rawfield and buried itself high in the wall of his chest.

Clew and Cromer Watts levelled their guns as one, but they were still too late. Wilf Bascoe, closer to Brady in many ways than the boy's father, was faster. His single bullet tore at Max Cargo's throat, sent him back over the rump of his horse, then to the ground in a gush of bright frothy blood.

But it wasn't enough for Bascoe. He watched horrified as Brady lost his grip on his saddle horn and crumpled sideways down to the ground. Methodically, he drew back the hammer of his gun, and fired. Then he did it again and again, twice more into Cargo's body. 'Damn you to Hell,' he seethed. 'He was no more'n a boy.'

'Somethin' there for each of us, I reckon,' Clew echoed Bascoe's sentiment.

Panic seized the three men who'd ridden with Cargo, and they were ready to break away whatever the cost.

Jesse's eyes hardly flickered as he warned them, 'Keep your guns, an' go. Head west an' don't stop for nothin' till you've crossed the Rockies.'

Clew was watching as Cargo's men rode away, then he holstered his Colt and climbed from the saddle.

Wilf Bascoe was kneeling on the ground,

his hand across Brady's forehead. 'He's breathin'. He's only still goddamn breathin',' he shouted heartily.

Clew had a close look, gave a testing measure of smile. 'Well, that usually means they ain't dead. The bullet must've missed somethin' vital. It does happen.'

'So we'll keep him alive,' Cromer Watts said, with a touch of cheer, as he too climbed down from his horse.

'We'll sure goddamn try,' Bascoe said. 'There won't be much left for any of us, if he don't make it. Not in Whisper.'

'We'll get him to the train,' Jesse contributed. 'If he ain't dead yet, he will be if he arrives there on horseback.'

Bascoe backed off a few steps, turned and lashed out at Cargo's body with his boot. 'If I'd just been that much quicker,' he said with quiet fury. Then he remounted his horse, sat forward of the horse's hips.

Clew and Watts carefully lifted Brady up to Bascoe's saddle.

'We'll follow on,' Clew said. 'Get him comfortable, an' tell Liam to keep up a head o' steam.'

When Clew and the others reached Blue Peak, they cut across the tracks in plain view of the timbermarkers' camp, but the place was now silent and deserted.

As fortune would have it, Austen Rawfield had hitched a ride on the footplate. Liam Baird had turned the engine on the reverse loop, and willing hands placed Brady securely and comfortably on the arm floor of the cab.

'Jesse, take these men up the slope an' find the sheriff,' Clew said. 'I'll be there later in the day with food an' blankets. I'd advise you to blockade the approach to the slope. If Stamper makes another move, you can stop him there an' then.'

Jesse nodded in understanding. 'If he tries, it'll say somethin' about his grit, if not his good sense. But I'll take care of it,' Jesse assured him. 'It's *you* that's got the hard job in facin' Milly.'

For twenty-four hours, Brady lay with a troubled fever in Doc Kelso's house. On more than one occasion, Wilf Bascoe suggested having the train make a mercy dash to Lima where Fort Garfield had an annexed hospital.

'His pa wants him taken home,' Kelso explained to them. 'I've located the bullet, an' it's not that far from his spine. It must have travelled along one of his ribs to get there.

There shouldn't be any immediate danger.'

It was another full day before he allowed Milly to see Brady. 'Wouldn't help his pulse rate,' he suggested drily.

Milly was too relieved that Brady was alive to be angry at anyone for his shooting, or to try and apportion blame. Austen Rawfield was just relieved.

Sensing Milly's fatigue, Clew went for the positive outcomes. 'Liam's replaced several damaged rails in the canyon,' he said. 'I knew you'd want to know as soon as Brady's condition improved. We've all suffered a crude intrusion, Milly, but now we can start over. We'll go up in the mornin' an' down in the evenin'. As for the telegraph, well there's just one wire I want you to send. Most other stuff we can handle between us. You go take care o' Brady for a while.'

'You believe we've got 'em licked? The Northern Pacific Rail Road?'

'I wouldn't go that far,' Clew said. 'But they might think twice before they make their next move.'

32

With Brady recovering, and two others who'd suffered serious injury, doing well, the Brannin faction could claim not to have lost a man. But Stamper hadn't been so lucky. Counting Max Cargo, three of his men had been killed, and so many wounded that he'd sent to Missoula for a railroad doctor.

In the late afternoon, Albie Cave rode up to the telegraph office. 'I've caught up on a few things,' Cave told Clew. 'I'm goin' down to spend a day or two with John Shallote. Any word you want to send him or Jesse?'

'Yeah, tell him we're back to service in the mornin'. Anyone up there then should listen for a real boisterous whistle.'

Cave nodded. 'That's good. By the way, I was talkin' to Dutch Barrow. He wants to know if you're collectin' damages from Stamper's company, over the blastin'?'

'Hah, an' wouldn't that be a waste o' time, Albie? They'd just say it weren't done on purpose, that it was an accident. We couldn't prove otherwise.'

Later, Clew spoke to Liam Baird about sending the morning train out on schedule.

'A schedule?' the engineer questioned. 'You mean a time?'

'Yeah, what else?'

'Well, in the past, if we had a customer ask what time the train left, we'd ask *them* what time they'd like.'

Clew smiled. But the train's timetable served a purpose, as far as Enoch Hudson and one or two other business folk were concerned. The so-called passenger accommodation remained unused. Clew guessed people were fearful that any future trouble might be repeated. But the lack of current business wasn't that important. He was waiting for a response to the wire Milly had sent for him.

The following evening Clew was waiting on the platform for the down train to pull in. There was a new passenger coach, and from it two men stepped down to the depot's jetty.

One of them had the air of importance that senior figures of big corporations appeared to gain with the years. It was exactly the look that Clew was hoping for. The other man appeared to be more inquisitive, more aware of fitting into his surroundings.

Rufus Maise smiled and held out his

hand. 'Clew,' he said, 'I'm sorry I couldn't get here a bit sooner. My business doesn't stop on a dime you know.'

Clew then shook hands with Hedley Yves, the reporter from the *Butte Examiner*. 'Thanks for comin'. You sure you don't know Sam Stamper ... that he don't know either o' you?' Clew wanted to know quickly.

Maise and Yves shook their heads. 'No, we've never met,' Maise confirmed. 'He'd be from the company's Bismark office.'

'Good, we'll get you over to Vine's an' signed in the book. That's the important thing. We'll sort out the detail from there. I want to be seen makin' real cosy with you two.'

Sitting in Rowan Vine's dining-room, Clew went through the detail of what he was after. 'Stamper will have a man or two on the lookout. The moment he gets to hear of an arrival in town, the registration details will be checked out. So, you're from Fort Bridger, not Helena or Butte City or anywhere north. You're both Union Pacific executives, an' I want every minute we're together lookin' like we're about to become partners in a great fat, rewardin' deal.'

'Just remind me of why I'm doing this?' Maise asked with a quizzical smile.

'Well, it was workin' for *you* that got us into this in the first place. Besides, you know what they say about all business an' no play?' Clew grinned back.

'And me?' Yves wanted to know.

'A great story,' Clew assured him.

Jesse came up that night to find Maise and Yves getting an account of the fight and the situation in general. He held in his surprise, as Clew made more information available and Maise made some suggestions for the next day.

'Do you reckon they already know you're here?' Jesse asked.

'We didn't advertise it,' Maise said. 'We brought a more comfortable car with us, but that was a matter of personal choice. Let's hope it's enough bait for your man to take.'

'Why didn't you tell me?' Jesse asked, as soon as the two would-be agents had retired for the night.

'It was hard not to, Jesse, but it was for all the best reasons. But it was *you* talked about the blue-funk, if an imaginary Union agent turned up. I thought so too ... just made it *less* imaginary.'

'Hmm. How much does Milly or anyone else know?'

'Nothin' more than the rumour that maybe there's an' interested party. But no one knows anythin' about it bein' the Union Pacific. They can work that out for themselves, an' my guess is, they already have. A sight of the Vine's register should confirm it.'

33

Clew was at the depot early to request that Liam Baird have the locomotive take them up to the Peak. Jesse wondered about the lack of surveying tools and instruments, but Maise pointed out that Hedley Yves and himself were playing the part of executives, not a work party. 'We're here looking at our investment, estimating the future, not banging in spikes.'

For an hour, the Brannin party wandered around, occasionally looking up and down the camp. To an interested observer, Maise and Yves appeared to be satisfied with what they saw. Every few minutes, they nodded and smiled encouragingly.

'What are *they* doin' up there?' Yves asked, on noticing the work that had already taken place above them on the ledge.

'They're takin' the road bed around the peak,' Clew replied. 'That's what we're meant to believe. But *two* can play the bluffin' game.'

'Ha. I think the trouble was not *them* doin' it, but *you* believin' they would,' Yves said. 'They must think you're true greenhorns. Christ, even I know that the first spring snow slide would butt everythin' off that ledge an' send it down here. An' if they put snow sheds up, you'd get matchwood. No, they ain't buildin' up there, fellers. It's back to square one. You got 'em stymied, an' I'm gettin' a good story.'

As Clew suspected, Sam Stamper had his scouts watching every move they made. The Northern Pacific man was sitting in his campaign tent waiting for news when one of his foremen came bustling in.

'They're here, boss,' he said. 'Two of 'em with the Brannins.'

By the time Stamper was in a position to see for himself, the Brannin locomotive was already on the down grade back to Whisper.

'Get a horse,' Stamper shouted angrily. 'You're ridin' to the next stop up the line. I've got to get a wire out.'

The locomotive pulled smoothly into the depot at Whisper. Jesse and Clew gave their thanks to Maise and Yves who in return expressed their amusement at the chimera, the appeal of taking part.

'Progress is a matter of public interest,' Yves said, 'and news of it is my concern.'

'Moreover, if I *was* a Union railroad man, I might think seriously about running a line up from Idaho Falls,' Maise said. 'There's broad profits to be made, and this little charade's *not* such a fanciful idea. You and your brother should think long term.'

'Ah, we got you to do that for us, Mr Maise,' Clew said inscrutably.

'I'll wager it won't be long before your Mr Stamper's got a lawyer back out here,' Maise continued and offered his hand. 'I'm heading straight back to Helena. That would be in keeping with someone having seen all they wanted to. Mr Yves is obviously staying for the full story.'

'Liam'll run you to Butte City. Seems the least we can offer, after you savin' our railroad an' all,' Jesse offered.

The remainder of the day was frustrating for Clew and Jesse. Especially as they weren't entirely out of the woods with their strategy, as well as keeping it from Milly Matches.

But that evening, and just as they'd hoped, Sam Stamper arrived at the depot to await the returning up train. When it pulled in, the first man down the steps was Noel Alliss, the well-known Missoula attorney.

'We got 'em,' Jesse said out of the corner of his mouth. 'They took the goddamn bait.'

Alliss saw them, and after conferring briefly with Stamper, he walked over. 'Remember me?' he started.

'Yeah, we turned down your fifty thousand-dollar offer,' Clew responded. 'Where's your friend? The one who offered us twenty-five?'

Alliss ignored the taunt. 'I came to do business with you an' Mr Stamper.'

'Good. Go ahead an' do it.'

'It looks like maybe you won your stonewall, Brannin. It's costin' too much to cut our own track, so to speak. So we've decided to accept your terms.'

'I wonder what brought you round to that?' Jesse said. 'Remind us of 'em.'

'We take the rail bed wherever we want, but it takes in your track, an' this town as part of the grand design.'

Clew nodded. 'Oh yeah, I remember now,' he said. 'But for one reason or another, the price has gone up.'

Alliss smiled coldly. 'I thought it might have done. There was a time when you weren't interested in the money, only your rail line.'

'Yeah, well, times change,' Jesse snapped.

'So what's your price? You've obviously not made any other commitment, or signed any papers at this point.'

'Not at this point, no,' Clew granted. 'But you know as well as we do, that we ain't all alone. An' now we know about values an' speculation. The price is two hundred thousand dollars, with a contract that obligates you to use the new Matches-Brannin Link. Oh, an' a pledge to rebuild Whisper and Hedley Yves gets an exclusive for the *Butte Examiner*.'

Alliss opened his briefcase. 'I've got the papers here,' he said with remarkable quickness. 'We only need a slight amendment.'

'What sort o' slight amendment?' Clew asked, as Alliss penned it in.

'The sum. We thought you'd go for a quarter-million. You just saved us fifty thousand dollars, Mr Brannin.'

There was a moment or two, while the interested parties settled their immediate thoughts.

Clew took off his hat and scratched his head. 'You're a tricky one, Mr Alliss. An' you got an interestin' way o' seein' through a deal,' he said, feeling both Jesse and Hedley Yves's suppressed laughter.

After the initial documents had been exchanged, Alliss looked apprehensively from Clew to Jesse, asked the question that was playing on his mind.

'Tell me, why didn't you sign on the line with those Union agents?'

'What Union agents?' Jesse said, looking innocent and non-plussed.

'What happens when they find out they got suckered?' Milly asked that night, as she sat with Clew and Jesse in the Vine's dining-room.

'Nothin'. We're about even on *that* score. Both sides got what they wanted,' Clew said.

'You're lookin' a bit happier than the last time we saw you, Milly,' Jesse observed. 'Welcome back the good times, eh?'

'There were some *recent* ones, when I was more worried about buyin' the next meal than keepin' the telegraph line open.'

Clew poured her a glass of French wine that Rowan had supplied. 'This is to new opportunities. You can live it up some now,' he said. 'You got the capital.'

'Apart from what I'm aimin' to blow on me

an' Brady's weddin' breakfast, what really happens to all that money?' Milly asked.

'We already told you. We take out our original stake o' seven thousand, an' another thousand for our trouble. *You* get to keep the rest. We retain our interest in the railroad, while you invest the balance. We'll take the same proportion o' shares, together with any risk. We're happy with that. Are you?'

'Yeah, who wouldn't be. Will McGirty says he's got enough tie-cuttin' work to last him ten years. Liam's already talkin' about a number two loco, a passenger car with carpets an' curtains, even.'

Clew grinned at the idea. 'Yeah, the country's grown' up, an' openin' out, Milly,' he said. 'You'll be able to go see some of it.'

'Where are you two goin'? You're obviously not stickin' around.'

'I don't think we ever intended to, Milly. Besides, Rufus Maise is goin' to squeeze us for bringin' him back here. There's always a price to pay somewhere.'

Jesse raised his glass. 'But it's the work we know. If you an' Brady ever find yourself in Bozeman, look us up. If it's trouble, it could be us who comes to sort it out.'

The publishers hope that this book has given you enjoyable reading. Large Print Books are especially designed to be as easy to see and hold as possible. If you wish a complete list of our books please ask at your local library or write directly to:

Dales Large Print Books
Magna House, Long Preston,
Skipton, North Yorkshire.
BD23 4ND